THE LAW
IN
COTTONWOOD

THE LAW
IN
COTTONWOOD

LEWIS B. PATTEN

G.K.HALL &CO.
Boston, Massachusetts
1982

Library of Congress Cataloging in Publication Data

Patten, Lewis B.
  The law in Cottonwood.

  "Published in large print"—Verso t.p.
  1. Large type books. I. Title.
[PS3566.A79L3 1982]   813'.54   82-9226
ISBN 0-8161-3365-4 (lg. print)   AACR2

Published in Large Print by arrangement with
Doubleday & Company, Inc.

Set in 18 pt English Times

THE LAW
IN
COTTONWOOD

CHAPTER 1

Morgan Gaunt awoke at dawn. For half a minute he lay still, listening. A rooster crowed faintly someplace uptown. Birds chirped in the big cottonwood outside the window of his room on the second floor of the Drovers Hotel. The town water wagon creaked past in the street below, sprinkling dusty Kansas Street in preparation for another day.

He swung his legs over the side of the bed and sat up. He wore only his underwear. His shoulders were broad and muscular, his chest deep, his belly flat.

He stood up and crossed the room to the washstand. He poured water into the basin and washed. Then he shaved and combed his dark, straight hair. He stroked his wide, full mustache a couple of times to make it lie in place, then put on a clean white shirt

1

and his black string tie. His pants came next, then his boots and then his worn brown vest. He picked up the massive gold watch from the dresser and put it into the lower right-hand pocket of the vest. The chain looped across the front, anchored by a gold penknife in the opposite pocket of the vest.

His holstered revolver on its cartridge belt came last. He buckled it around his waist and it settled snugly against his right hip where his pants were worn shiny by its movement as he walked.

He took his wide-brimmed black hat from the coat tree beside the door and settled it on his head. He went out, then closed and locked the door and pocketed the key. He descended the stairs and crossed the deserted lobby with only a quick glance at the sleeping clerk behind the desk. He stepped out onto the long veranda into the yellow glow of the rising sun. Its rays struck the gleaming six-pointed marshal's star pinned to the upper left-hand pocket of his vest.

He stood at the edge of the veranda and let his glance run up and down the street. Nothing moved except for the water wagon, now returning from the depot at the lower end of town. From his shirt pocket, Gaunt took a Bull Durham sack, separated a wheatstraw paper from the pack and shook some flakes of tobacco into it. He rolled the smoke, licked it, then twisted the ends and stuck it into his mouth. He scratched a match alight on one of the round white posts that supported the veranda roof, in a place scarred by hundreds of other similar scratches, and touched it to the cigarette. He drew smoke into his lungs, stepped down into the street and started diagonally across heading toward the livery barn three blocks down.

The smell of dampened dust was strong in the air, mingling with the elusive fragrance of lilacs and of fresh-cut grass hay from beyond the upper edge of town. The early air was warm. Another hot one, he thought.

A block from the hotel, the water wagon passed. Luke Matty, driving, raised a hand and spoke respectfully, his soft words indistinguishable because of the clatter and squeak of the wagon wheels. Gaunt returned the greeting and continued toward the livery barn.

It was deserted. Elwood Hooker, the stableman, did not come to work until seven. Gaunt walked back to his horse's stall and led the tall chestnut out. He saddled him, mounted and rode down the inclined wooden ramp into the street.

Now he was complete, a big man on a big horse, the law in Cottonwood. He headed down toward the depot and the cattle pens beyond, beginning his morning rounds.

His horse's hoofs were muffled in the deep, damp dust of the street, but they clattered as the horse stepped up onto the station platform and went past the station to the telegrapher's cubbyhole at its farthest end. The telegrapher, Jim Sutton, glanced up at the familiar sound and raised a hand in greeting as Gaunt went by.

A sign on the depot, facing east, proclaimed that this was Cottonwood, Kansas, Population 412. Adjacent to the station were the cattle pens, stretching away for nearly half a mile. In another day or two they'd be full of bawling, dusty cattle, waiting their turn at the loading chutes. Out on the prairie to the east and west and south would be tens of thousands more, bunched and held and waiting too.

And instead of 412 persons, Cottonwood would hold a thousand or more, the increase composed of wild and lean and sun-baked Texas cowboys who had brought the great herds up the trail. They were one reason the town needed Morgan Gaunt. They were one reason the town paid him a hundred and fifty dollars a month, winter and summer, even though he was needed less than half that time.

The cowboys drew another element; gamblers, saloonkeepers, prostitutes and thieves. They were an added reason the town needed Morgan Gaunt.

He rode at a steady walk down the center alley between the cattle pens and beyond, into the tree-and-brush-grown bed of Cottonwood Creek. He followed its course along the eastern edge of town.

At the upper town limits, he climbed his horse out of the creek bed where Elwood Hooker's hayfields lay bare and freshly cut in the growing heat of the morning sun. A buck rake stood at the edge of one field, along with a rusty dump rake and a wagon with a hayrack on it.

He skirted Hooker's fields, which were fenced with barbed Glidden wire, then entered town again at its upper end on Kansas Street. He could see Matty's water wagon still creaking along the dusty street, but nothing else moved yet.

Up here were the tall, white, coolly

shaded homes of the town's wealthy and prominent citizens—Lester Ives, who owned the bank, Sam Kohn, who owned the Cottonwood Mercantile and Kurt Vossler, who owned five of the town's eleven saloons.

Smaller and less-imposing homes stretched along Kansas Street farther down, and on Maple and Oak, which paralleled Kansas Street on either side.

Pacing his horse slowly, he rode along through two blocks of comfortable residences, all of which had both chicken houses and stables at the rear, most of which had vegetable gardens and berry bushes someplace on their premises. The smell of lilacs was stronger here, and the tall bushes, heavy with blossom clusters, were present in nearly every yard.

A couple of dogs walked out and barked at him, wagging their tails as they did. It was a ritual with the two dogs, both of which he knew by name. A good-natured greeting they gave him every day. He spoke to them and they stopped barking, followed him a hundred yards or so, still lazily wagging their tails, then halted, sat down and scratched.

A couple of more blocks between Second

Street and Main contained even more modest homes, some of these needing repair. Then the town's business section began with the huge, hundred-room Cattlemen's Hotel at the corner of Kansas Street and Main and the Cottonwood Bank across the street. Next to it on the south was the Cottonwood Mercantile, a store that handled everything from lumber to dry goods, from groceries to guns. Other smaller stores lined Kansas Street between Main and Texas streets, and on the northwest corner of Texas and Kansas stood the Drovers Hotel where Gaunt had his room.

Texas Street was the deadline above which the cowboys were forbidden to come. Most of them didn't want to come north of Texas Street, but every year there were a few who had to challenge anything that restricted them. Gaunt handled them swiftly and efficiently, and they usually wound up in jail unhurt but chastened and willing in the future to abide by the rule.

Gaunt understood Texans, perhaps better than they understood themselves. They weren't mean, only exuberant and fiercely independent. He gave them the respect they felt they were entitled to, and in return most of them avoided breaking any of the rules

7

laid down by the town council and enforced by Gaunt.

A Negro in a white coat was sweeping the veranda of the Cattlemen's Hotel. He spoke to Gaunt, and the marshal returned the greeting. Along this block the businesses stood locked and empty at this early hour. Gaunt rode up on the board sidewalk a couple of times to try a door without getting off his horse. He could smell coffee brewing as he passed the Drovers Hotel.

Nine of the town's eleven saloons were in the next block lining both sides of the street. Largest and most imposing was the Alamo, which had leaded, stained-glass windows depicting a herd of cattle on one side of the doors, a bucking horse and rider on the other. Heavy outer doors were pad-locked over the inner swinging doors, and Gaunt's glance automatically checked the padlock before he went on. The town's remaining two saloons were on Goliad, along with dingy shops that catered to the cowboys and drovers. Beyond Goliad, on Kansas, Maple and Oak were the brothels, mostly run-down, tarpaper shacks with bare, unkempt yards, in each of which one or two girls worked.

Two weeks ago, this area had been nearly

deserted. Gaunt didn't know where the girls came from or where they worked during the winter. But they always came back a couple of weeks before the arrival of the first cattle herd.

All eleven of the saloons were open for business now, every day. All that was needed was the first cattle herd to get things rolling for another year.

Gaunt finished his patrol at the stone jail next to the livery barn. He dismounted and tied his horse in the shade of a box elder tree at the north side of the jail. He unlocked the door and went inside.

He knew his job was dangerous. Every year he laid his life on the line at least a dozen times, to say nothing of minor skirmishes, any one of which could become deadly suddenly and unexpectedly.

He accepted the danger along with the hundred and fifty dollars a month. He was fatalistic, and because he was it was said of him that he knew no fear.

That wasn't so. Every time he walked into a darkened alley to disarm a drunken cowboy who was threatening to kill him, he felt fear as a high tension in his chest, an emptiness in his belly, invisible but very real tremors in his hands and knees.

But there was a fine, high exhilaration in those deadly moments, a stimulus he never felt at any other time. This kept him on the job, a job that often angered and sometimes disgusted him.

He crossed the room to his desk in the center of it, sat down and lifted his booted feet to the desk. The clock on the wall said twenty minutes after six.

The hotel dining room would open at seven. Until then he had nothing to do.

He thought about Buck Robineau. Sometime in the next few days Robineau would be bringing another herd up the trail. Before his crew loaded him on a wagon for the long trip south last year, Robineau had sworn to return this year and kill Morgan Gaunt.

He raised his head at the sound of a horse galloping up the street from the direction of the railroad tracks. He got up, crossed to the door and opened it.

The heat in the street was already considerable, at least ten degrees hotter than the inside of the jail. He stepped outside.

The rider was a tow-headed boy of about thirteen, riding a barebacked horse. He saw the marshal and yelled, "Marshal! They're here! The first herd is here!"

The boy was Leon Satterfield, whose father had a small farm a dozen miles south of town. He pulled his horse to a plunging halt and slid off his back.

Morgan took half a dollar from his pocket and tossed it to Leon. He could see that Leon was waiting for him to ask who the trail boss was and he suppressed a smile. Finally Leon said excitedly, "It ain't Buck Robineau. It's somebody I ain't never seen before."

Gaunt nodded. "Thanks, Leon. You must've left before it got light."

"I did. I left as soon as I got up. They're camped about a mile west of our place. They pulled in last night. I rode over there and talked to 'em. I knew you'd want to know who it was."

Gaunt nodded. Leon hesitated several moments, then glanced uptown toward the Kansas Mercantile. The fifty cents was burning a hole in his pocket, Gaunt thought. He'd probably take home a quarter and tell his pa that was all he'd got. He'd spend the other quarter on candy at the store.

Finally Leon asked, "You goin' out there today?"

"Likely will, after breakfast. You want to

11

ride with me?"

"Sure, Mr. Gaunt. I'll meet you in front of the hotel." He went on up the street, and stopped in front of the Kansas Mercantile. He tied his horse, then sat down on the steps to wait.

Gaunt stood motionless on the boardwalk in front of the jail. People were beginning to come into the street, children to play or run errands for their folks, adults to open the various stores on Kansas Street.

Gaunt waited idly for a while, watching the town stir and come to life. Finally, judging it was near seven, he turned and locked the jail door, then walked slowly up the street toward the Drovers Hotel.

He could smell coffee again before he reached the door. He climbed the steps and went in. The desk clerk was awake. Gaunt turned and crossed the white-tile floor to the dining room. He took his accustomed table at the window. Sunlight flooded in, not yet hot enough to be uncomfortable.

A pretty young Mexican girl brought him coffee. "Good morning, Marshal Gaunt."

"Good morning, Josephina. I'll have a steak. And about three eggs."

"Yes, sir." She hesitated, and he knew she had seen Leon sitting on the steps across the street and had guessed why he was in town. Finally she asked, "Is the first herd here?"

He nodded. "Got in last night, according to Leon."

She nodded and went away. Gaunt sipped the hot black coffee as he waited for her to return with his meal.

He was glad the first herd was here. He was glad that he would now have something to do and could earn his pay. He didn't like the idle winter months of sitting in his office at the jail or in one of the saloons.

But there was a complication this year that had not been the case last year. The town council had passed an ordinance forbidding firearms inside the town limits. Signs had been posted on all roads leading into town, and it was to advise the newly arrived drovers of this new ordinance that Gaunt intended to ride out to the herd south of town today.

It would make trouble, that was sure. For some reason a Texas cowboy didn't feel dressed without his gun. Gaunt had opposed the ordinance, but he had been overruled.

Josephina brought him a steak, three eggs and a generous helping of fried

13

potatoes, as well as biscuits, butter and jam. She refilled his coffee cup and he began to eat.

CHAPTER 2

At eight, Gaunt rode out of town on his tall chestnut, accompanied by Leon Satterfield. The boy looked a little sick and Gaunt knew he had stuffed himself with candy from the store. In a way the boy was like the Texas drovers who, when they hit town after three hard months on the trail, couldn't seem to fill themselves with liquor fast enough. They always ended up sick, too, but they never learned. Next time it was the same story all over again.

They clattered over the bridge at the lower end of town and rode out onto the rolling grassland, following the narrow, dusty road that petered out into a trail about ten miles south of town.

Leon watched Gaunt surreptitiously for a while, but finally he blurted out, "What you reckon them cowboys will do when

15

you tell 'em they can't wear guns to town?''

Gaunt smiled faintly. ''They'll bluster and raise hell and swear no cow-town marshal is going to tell them what to do, but in the end they'll come to town without their guns.''

''What if they don't?''

''Then I'll have to take their guns away from them.''

Gaunt knew that the success of the ordinance against guns would depend largely on what happened today. If he enforced it with these first arrivals, those from the herds that followed would accept it more easily. Even so, there would be plenty of die-hards who had to be convinced.

He let the chestnut lope for several miles until the animal's hide gleamed with sweat. Then he drew back on the reins and afterward held the horse to a steady, mile-eating trot. The chestnut didn't get much exercise so when he did get out of town, Gaunt usually let him run off his head of steam.

It was nearly ten when he sighted the cloud of dust ahead. Ten minutes later he sighted the point rider, with the herd leaders immediately behind. He turned his horse and rode off to the windward side for

16

several hundred yards. Waiting, he fished out his Bull Durham sack and rolled himself a smoke.

Point rider and herd leaders passed, followed by the strung-out herd. The cattle were trail-wise now, after three months, and they plodded along patiently with a minimum of jostling. Three men detached themselves from the flank and approached.

The first thing their eyes caught was the star on Morgan Gaunt's vest. The man in the lead was spare and stringy, maybe five-feet-ten. His hair was gray and his week's growth of whiskers also had a liberal sprinkling of gray. His hat was dusty, shapeless, with a wide, stained band around the crown where sweat had soaked clear through. His eyes were gray, emotionless and direct. His mouth was a thin line untouched by any smile. Gaunt said, "I'm the marshal of Cottonwood."

"Heard of you." The man's voice was hoarse and unemotional.

Gaunt said, "Welcome to Cottonwood. Yours is the first herd to arrive, so you'll get first crack at the pens. There's a hundred and fifty cars or thereabouts on a siding east of town."

The man nodded.

Gaunt said, "I didn't get your name."

"Wedemeier. Nick Wedemeier. This is a pool herd. Six hundred head. Two hundred of 'em are mine."

Gaunt said, "Your boys are welcome in town. We'll try to show 'em a good time. But there's a new ordinance. No guns in town. It'll be enforced."

Wedemeier scowled and seemed about to argue the point. He changed his mind. "I'll tell 'em," was all he said.

He and the two men with him reined their horses around and trotted back toward the herd.

Leon said, "Not very friendly, is he?"

"He's been three months on the trail. He's likely had nothing but trouble all the way. Now I'm bringing him some more. You can't expect him to like it much."

"You think his cowboys will come to town without their guns?"

"No. They'll come in *with* their guns. It will be a test to see if I can make the gun ban stick." He had hoped it would be different. He had hoped the first trail boss would be a more reasonable kind of man. This Wedemeier would simply tell his cowboys about the ordinance and let it go at that. He wouldn't order them to comply.

Leon looked as if he'd like to accompany the marshal back to town. He knew he couldn't, though, so he said good-bye and turned his horse toward home.

Gaunt urged the chestnut to a trot and headed back toward town. He passed the slowly moving herd and arrived in town before noon.

The streets were crowded now. Once more he tied the chestnut in the shade of the box elder tree beside the jail and walked uptown to the Alamo Saloon.

The town council had offered to hire two deputy marshals at the time they passed the ordinance banning guns. Gaunt had refused. Deputies would only get themselves killed trying to enforce such an ordinance. Gaunt could do it but only because he was known to the Texas cattlemen and their friends. He was known to be tough and uncompromising and was believed to be fearless. He was also conceded to be fair. It added up to "presence," although Gaunt had never thought about it just that way. He personified the law, and the law was only as strong as the man enforcing it.

The saloon was crowded for this time of day. Men made way for him, and he slowly worked his way through them to the bar.

He ordered beer and the brimming mug came sliding down the bar to stop exactly in front of him. He laid down a nickel and picked up the beer.

He felt the soft touch of a woman's hand on his arm and turned his head to see Rose Navarro standing at his side. "Hello, Morgan."

"Hello, Rose." The smile that touched his wide and normally sombre mouth held genuine warmth.

"I hear the first herd is here." She was a small, dark-haired woman with ample breasts, a slender waist and full, rounded hips. She was Morgan Gaunt's girl, and because she was other men left her alone. Which suited her. She owned a one-fourth share in the Alamo.

"Uh-huh. They'll be in town tonight."

She knew about the weapons ordinance, but she didn't mention it. She said, "Things will be quiet this afternoon. Come up and visit for a while." Her eyes were warm and personal.

He understood what the invitation included and nodded. He had known her three years, ever since he had come to Cottonwood and taken the marshal's job. He'd never talked with her about his past, and she had never discussed hers with him. She knew he was courting Maggie Conover and knew there could be no future in her own relationship with him. She doubted if Maggie Conover knew about her. She also doubted if Maggie would continue seeing him if she did.

With just a trace of weariness in her voice she said, "Another year."

"You could sell out and do something else. Your share of this place will never be worth more than it is right now."

"And what would I do?"

"How about nothing?" He grinned. "How about keeping house?"

Her smile matched his. "For you?"

His own grin faded, and she was sorry she had embarrassed him. She squeezed his arm. "See you this afternoon."

"Sure."

Morgan went out into the sun-washed street. The heat was building up. Dust rose now in spite of the street's two earlier sprinklings.

It was past noon and time to eat. He headed for Maggie Conover's restaurant, thinking of her and smiling at his thoughts.

He saw nothing inconsistent in his relationships with Maggie and with Rose, although he knew Maggie would not be tolerant if she knew. He was a mature man, and his periodic need for a woman was real and undeniable. Maggie, although she had been married before, was firm in her conviction that intimacy with a man must be preceded by marriage. He had been trying to get her to marry him, but she would not do so until her husband had been dead a year.

Her restaurant was sandwiched in-between the bank and the Cottonwood Mercantile. Already it was nearly filled with customers. There was a vacant stool at the end of the counter near the swinging door that led to the kitchen, and he sat down on it. As he did, Maggie came through the door, carrying four plates with practiced dexterity. She saw him and the way her face lighted made him feel good. She said, "Morgan! I'll be right back."

He smiled, one of his rare, complete smiles, and its warmth made her already flushed face flush more. She went on past and carried the plates to a table by the window occupied by four of the town's businessmen.

Morgan turned his head to watch her. He liked the way she walked, her back straight, her head high, her hips moving naturally but very beautifully. Turning, she caught his glance and a faint smile touched her mouth.

She was taller than Rose, with smaller breasts and a more slender figure, probably from the hard work involved in running the restaurant. Her hair was dark, done up in a bun at the nape of her neck, with wisps of it escaping the restraint and lying now damp on her forehead and neck.

She stopped beside him, laid a hand on his arm and asked, "What will you have, Morgan?"

"Wasn't that chicken and dumplings you just carried by?"

She nodded.

"Then I'll have some of that."

She said, "I can't talk now. Too busy. But stay awhile. This will clear out in a little while."

He nodded and she disappeared into the kitchen. On her next trip out she brought him a cup of coffee and half a dozen trips later brought him a steaming plate of chicken and dumplings and refilled his coffee cup.

He ate, frowning slightly, thinking about Nick Wedemeier and about Wedemeier's crew. He hoped he wouldn't have to start off the year by throwing anyone in jail or by being forced to draw his gun.

Wedemeier would hold his herd a mile or two from town tonight. He'd come in to talk to the cattle buyers and, if they reached a satisfactory agreement, would make arrangements for cattle cars tomorrow. He'd accept an advance from whoever bought his cattle, and would give his cowboys at least a part of their pay. The cowboys themselves would hit town around dark, and Morgan Gaunt would begin to earn his pay again.

Gradually the restaurant emptied until, at a little after one, Gaunt was the only one who remained. Maggie brought a cup of coffee and sat down limply on the stool next to him. Her forehead was damp and wisps of her dark hair clung to it.

Her face was lovely, he thought, as he looked at her. Her forehead was high and smooth, her eyes large and dark and widely spaced. Her cheekbones were high, her mouth full and her chin strong. She said, "I like to have you look at me like that."

"Then I'll do it more."

Her smile faded. "I hear the first herd is here."

He nodded.

"Will they obey the order not to bring guns to town?"

"Maybe."

"And if they don't?" She knew the answer to that, but she wanted to be reassured that he could handle it.

"I'll have to change their minds."

She was silent for several moments, her eyes studying his face. Finally she asked, "You'll be careful, won't you Morgan?"

"Yes." He was always careful, never reckless. He never did anything impulsively, but he could act, when it was necessary, with cold ruthlessness that had gained him the respect, if not the liking, of all the Texans who had happened to cross paths with him.

The cloud remained on her face as she sipped her coffee. He reached out and covered her hand, lying on the counter, with his own. She looked up, met his glance and asked, "Will Buck Robineau be coming back this year?"

"He said he would." Morgan's clash with Robineau last year had been over the jailing of one of the members of Robineau's crew. Robineau had come to the jail with a dozen members of his crew to get the man out. Morgan hadn't had any choice. It was give up the cowboy and lose all the control he had in Cottonwood, or duel it out with Robineau. He'd chosen the latter course and had severely wounded Robineau, who had lain in a room at the Cattlemen's Hotel five weeks before he was sufficiently recovered to make the trip back to Texas in a spring wagon bed.

Before he left, he confronted the marshal with the promise that he would return this year and kill Morgan any way he could. Which meant, since his right shoulder had been smashed by Morgan's bullet, that he'd probably not do it in a man-to-man, face-to-face gun duel.

Maggie asked, "Why don't you quit this job? Before . . ." She didn't finish but he knew what she had been going to say.

He thought about it a moment before he answered her. He knew it was only a matter of time before one of the bullets fired at him from out of the darkness found its mark. Or before he miscalculated about whether some drunken cowboy would draw his gun and paid for his miscalculation with his life.

Besides, he knew the life of Cottonwood as a cattle town was limited. The herds would stop coming here just as they had stopped coming to Baxter Springs, Ellsworth, Newton and Wichita. And a sleepy farm town would have neither need for his talents nor the funds to pay for them.

He thought about the alternatives, about the jobs he might get, and he rejected all of them. The only thing that might satisfy him would be owning his own ranch, and he knew even that would be pretty dull by comparison. But Maggie was waiting for his answer and he said, "I've always been a lawman. Ever since the war. What would I do?"

He could see that she was thinking too. Of him behind the counter of this restaurant. Or running a store, selling dress goods and hardware and groceries. He didn't fit the mold, and a fleeting smile at the incongruity of it touched her mouth. She said, "There are things. You could start a freight line. Or drive a stagecoach. Or buy a cattle ranch."

He said, "I'll think about it."

There was something speculative in her expression. She was probably considering making his changing jobs a condition of their marrying. But she had the good sense not to issue any ultimatums or impose any conditions. He was not a man to be coerced.

She nodded. "All right." But there was a cloud in her eyes, a worry that, even if she did persuade him to quit after the Texas cowboys had all gone home and the town was quiet again, it might not be soon enough.

He was faced with enforcing the gun ban, not only against the cowboys from the herd that would arrive later today, but against all those who would come afterward. He was faced with enforcing the two-o'clock curfew when not one of the saloonkeepers approved of it. He was faced with the threat made by Buck Robineau to return this year and kill him by whatever means were necessary. He might not live to quit even if he agreed to do so at the end of the year.

But she could not change this man. He was committed to serving out this year at least. Nothing would make him quit.

Besides, she thought as she looked at his strong and flat-planed face, he didn't really want to quit. He liked the job. He liked the excitement of risking his life every day and every night.

She wondered bleakly if women ever completely understood their men. She doubted if they did.

CHAPTER 3

Morgan Gaunt walked into the Alamo at two-thirty. He drank a beer at the bar, then crossed the room, in which there were now only half a dozen men, and climbed the stairs.

There was a balcony up here, with doors leading to the various rooms where the saloon girls took their customers. Rose Navarro's room was down at the end.

Morgan knocked and when Rose's voice called, "Come in, Morgan," he entered, struck as he always was by the frilly femininity of this room.

She was dressed in something gauzey that gave him just a hint of white skin underneath. He felt his blood stir and his heart begin to pound. She got up and poured him a drink from the bottle on the table. He took it from her and sipped. He said, "You're a damned beautiful woman, Rose."

She wanted to ask him if she was more beautiful than Maggie Conover, but she had the good sense to keep still. She poured herself a drink and extended it far enough toward him to touch his glass. Afterward she drank about half of it.

How long would she have him? she wondered to herself. Would he really marry Maggie when her year of mourning was up, or would he shy away? He had apparently shied away before because he was past thirty and as far as she knew had never been married.

Or had he? That was something she simply didn't know because neither of them had ever discussed the past. It occurred to her that if she arranged to let Maggie find out about their relationship, she might end his relationship with Maggie Conover. But she immediately discarded that idea. Rose had spent all her adult life in saloons, but she had a rigid honesty that wouldn't permit her to stoop to such tactics even to get Morgan, who she wanted more than she had ever wanted anything or anyone.

She finished her drink and Morgan finished his. He got up and came to her, and took her in his arms. He was very direct as he always was, but there was a tenderness in him too that moved her today just as it always had in the past.

Yet throughout, she had the feeling that a part of him was someplace else, and she supposed he was thinking of the herd out on the prairie south of town and of the gun ban he would have to enforce tonight. He was wondering, also, if he would have to kill a man, and maybe he was wondering if he would be killed himself, although she doubted that.

He stayed with her for about an hour, then got up and dressed himself and belted on his gun. With his hat in his hand, he bent and kissed her lightly on the mouth. She was so touched by this gentle kiss that said so much that for a moment tears glistened in her eyes. Then he was gone and she could hear the beat of his booted heels on the balcony and later on the stairs.

She supposed she should be grateful for having had as much of him as she had, yet womanlike, she wanted more. She wanted to have all of him, forever, the way Maggie Conover would when she married him.

But Rose was a realist. She had given up all chance for marriage and children and the permanence both bring a woman when she went to work in her first saloon. She had been sixteen at the time although she had looked older, and she hadn't made a conscious decision to give up one thing for another or even known what she might be giving up. Her decision had been dictated by circumstances. Her parents had been killed in a stagecoach wreck. She hadn't been able to find a job to support herself. A saloon had been the only alternative.

Slowly she dressed for the evening, taking her time, occasionally smiling faintly as her thoughts dwelt on Morgan Gaunt. Finished, she descended the stairs, ready for another night.

Here in the Alamo she would soon know whether Morgan had successfully enforced the new gun ban. And she would be among the first to know if anything went wrong.

Kurt Vossler was a huge, grossly fat man in his early fifties. He wore a neatly trimmed Van Dyke beard and mustache. His eyes were close-set, baby-blue in color and nearly lost in the folds of fat surrounding them. They were as hard and dangerous as the eyes of a full-grown boar.

Vossler owned five of the town's eleven

saloons and one of the three imposing mansions at the upper end of town. Vossler's saloons were the sleaziest of the eleven. They were also places where anything went, and because they were, they always had a crowd.

Vossler hated Gaunt more than he had ever hated anyone. He blamed Gaunt for the two-o'clock closing ordinance. Gaunt was always there when two o'clock rolled around, ordering Vossler's bartenders to close, and the marshal was always trying to get Vossler on some trumped-up charge, although so far all he had succeeded in getting against Vossler had been misdemeanors that resulted in fines.

He kept on trying though, trying to prove that Vossler knew about the cowboy drunks that went off with Vossler's girls and ended up in the alley with their pockets turned inside out and, often as not, bad lumps on their heads. A few had even died as a result of their injuries, and Gaunt had told Vossler straight out that he knew he was behind the killings and that, sooner or later, he was going to prove it and see that Vossler hanged.

Vossler's direct mind saw only one solution to the problem posed by Morgan

Gaunt. The marshal had to go. Sometime this year maybe he would find a man willing to kill Gaunt, someone who had a grievance of his own strong enough to make him forget the risk. When he did, Morgan Gaunt would be gone for good. The gun ban and the closing ordinance would be forgotten and Vossler would start running his saloons the way he wanted to. Hell, this cattle boom wasn't going to last more than another couple of years. The other hell-raising cow towns east of here were dying on the vine. Herds no longer came to them. They had to depend on farmers to keep them alive.

Vossler meant to get all he could before that happened in Cottonwood. And he wasn't doing bad. He had his house at the upper end of town. He had five saloons. He had a sizable amount of money in the bank.

But when this town died, the saloons wouldn't be worth the powder to blow them to hell. The house wouldn't be worth much more. He'd made a few investments, but he wanted more. The next two years ought to put him on easy street. Provided Gaunt didn't spoil everything.

Today, Vossler left home at noon. He

drove his buggy down Kansas Street to the first of his saloons—the Red Dog on the corner of Kansas and Goliad. The bartender, a hard-faced man named Sully, came out and helped him alight. He went inside and Sully followed him. Sully said, "The first herd's here, Mr. Vossler. Things ought to pick up tonight."

"Who's the trail boss, Sully? Do you know?"

Sully shook his head. "No, sir."

"Then it probably isn't Robineau, or you'd have heard."

"Yes, sir. I suppose I would."

Vossler sat down at one of the tables and Sully brought him one of his private bottles and a glass. Vossler decided he'd have to wait until Robineau came. Maybe Robineau would get rid of Gaunt and save him the trouble and the risk. If he didn't . . . well, there would be time enough then to hire somebody to do the job.

Or it might get done without him having to take any action at all. It might happen tonight when Gaunt tried enforcing the gun ban on the cowhands who had just arrived.

The thing to do was to relax. Things have a way of taking care of themselves.

After leaving Maggie Conover's restaurant Gaunt had made his rounds for the second time today. The midday inspection was the one he enjoyed the most. A lot of people were on the street and he stopped often to talk with someone for a few minutes, about the weather or the number of cattle likely to be shipped east out of Cottonwood this year or something else of little consequence.

He saw Vossler's buggy in front of the Red Dog, but he did not go in. When he left Rose at the Alamo at three-thirty and saw Vossler's buggy still in the same place, he turned in through the Red Dog's swinging doors.

Vossler's five saloons caused him more trouble than all the others combined. Vossler hired only crooked gamblers, and since the house shared in every game, this increased his take. Gaunt knew in his own mind that Vossler encouraged his girls to roll drunken cowboys every chance they got, and he was sure Vossler got his share of whatever they took from their victims.

Cheating and robbing the Texans was bad enough. But what really angered Gaunt was the fact that all too often the blow intended to render the victim unconscious killed him instead. It had happened three times last year. Gaunt meant to see that it didn't happen at all this year.

Vossler was sitting at a table, a bottle of his special whiskey in front of him. Sully, a hard case Gaunt never turned his back to if he could help it, was behind the bar.

Gaunt stood over Vossler, ignoring Vossler's invitation to sit down.

He said, "The first herd is here, Mr. Vossler."

Vossler nodded. "I heard." He studied Gaunt's face as if trying to read Gaunt's thoughts.

Gaunt said, "Clean up your places, Mr. Vossler, or I'll close them. A violation of the law in one, and I'll close all five."

Vossler's fat face flushed darkly and his tiny eyes glittered. He said softly, "You son-of-a-bitch, try closing me and you'll be dead before the night's over."

Gaunt's expression didn't change. He couldn't arrest Vossler for calling him a son-of-a-bitch, and if he arrested him for the threat, he'd never make it stick. Not with Sully the only witness to the threat. Besides, arresting Vossler on a minor charge would only lay him open to an accusation of harassment later on when he got something serious on the man.

He stared at Vossler, his face composed but with a dark anger in the depths of his eyes. Vossler opened his mouth to curse Gaunt again. Something he saw in Gaunt's eyes changed his mind. Gaunt said, "Remember it. One crooked game, one drunk rolled, and you're closed for ten days. All five."

"By God I'll see the town council about that!"

"See them." Gaunt turned his back and went to the door. He knew either Sully or Vossler was capable of shooting him in the back. But not like this. Not when there was no one else to blame it on.

He stepped out on the boardwalk. The heat was heavy and oppressive now. The sprinkling wagon was wetting down Kansas street for the third time today.

Gaunt saw the trail boss, Nick Wedemeier, on the veranda of the Cattlemen's Hotel with a cattle buyer named Bart Chapman, the banker, Lester Ives, and Dave Ryan, who worked for the AT&SF railroad. As he watched, the quartet stepped down off the hotel veranda, crossed the street and entered the Cottonwood Bank.

Wedemeier had made his deal, thought Gaunt. He'd be returning to his herd with an advance, and his cowboys would hit town less than an hour afterward.

He meant to meet them at the edge of town. He figured he'd have his best chance before any of them had gotten anything to drink. They'd be anxious to hit the saloons and they'd be thinking about the girls. They'd be less likely to make an issue of their guns than they would later on.

Wedemeier came out of the bank, now accompanied only by the buyer, Chapman, and the railroad man, Ryan. He stood talking with them on the walk in front of the bank for several minutes. Then he untied his horse, mounted and came down the street.

Gaunt mounted his own horse and when Wedemeier came abreast, fell in beside him. "Make a deal for your herd, Mr. Wedemeier?"

Wedemeier looked pleased. He nodded.

"When will you load?"

"Day after tomorrow. I don't figure my men will be much good tomorrow."

Gaunt grinned faintly. "You're likely right."

Wedemeier didn't seem to have anything else to say. Gaunt sensed a hidden hostility in the man, and since Wedemeier didn't know him he supposed Wedemeier had heard about him from others who did. He said, "Your boys will be treated fairly, Mr. Wedemeier. You have my word for that."

Wedemeier looked at him but still he didn't speak. He nodded to signify that he accepted Gaunt's statement as the truth, at least until future events proved otherwise.

"You'll save everybody a lot of trouble if you send 'em to town without their guns."

Wedemeier glanced at him, an unsuccessfully hidden mockery in his eyes. "Afraid of them, Mr. Gaunt?"

Gaunt said, "You've heard about me, Mr. Wedemeier. Did you hear that I was afraid?"

Wedemeier reluctantly shook his head. But the stubborn look remained. "I can't send them in without their guns. How the hell are they going to protect themselves?"

"I'm here to protect them, Mr. Wedemeier."

Wedemeier shook his head. "You'll have to get their guns the best way you can. If I send them in unarmed and one of them gets killed . . ." He left the sentence dangling.

Gaunt saw that he had lost. He shrugged,

drew in his horse's reins and stopped. He watched Wedemeier cross the railroad tracks and take the narrow road leading south.

He hadn't really expected the trail boss to send his men in without their guns. But he'd had to try.

He rode back to the jail. He took the bit out of his horse's mouth and tied up the reins. He released the horse beneath the box elder tree to graze. There was a vacant lot between the jail and Sandoval's Saddle Shop. It was ankle high with dry native grass.

He brought a straight-backed chair from inside the jail and placed it on the walk. He sat down and tilted it back against the wall. The sinking sun beat hot against him and he tilted his hat forward to keep it out of his eyes. He began to sweat from the heat, but he didn't move.

Glancing up the street now, he could see that he wasn't the only one who had seen Wedemeier leave town. Girls appeared in the windows and on the porches of the tarpaper brothels, painted and provocatively dressed. Gamblers in cutaway coats and black hats drifted from the two hotels into the various saloons. Bartenders and swampers came to work.

Kurt Vossler came out of the Red Dog and waddled out of sight on Goliad, no doubt visiting the remaining four of his five saloons. He reappeared about twenty minutes later, climbed heavily into his buggy and drove away toward home, throwing only a hasty glance toward the marshal sitting in front of the jail.

Gaunt thought idly that he had better be more careful than usual this year. Vossler wanted him out of the way, and while he probably didn't have the guts to try killing him himself, he could have it done.

The sun settled toward the horizon. An hour after Wedemeier had ridden out of town, Gaunt walked to where his horse was cropping grass. He put the bit back into the horse's mouth, mounted and rode down Kansas Street.

He watered his horse in Cottonwood Creek, then took up a position south of the bridge to wait.

CHAPTER 4

Waiting, he thought of Maggie Conover, and then about Rose. He couldn't help feeling guilty about seeing Rose and courting Maggie at the same time, and he felt sure that if Maggie knew about Rose she would break off with him at once.

But he wasn't a priest, and he couldn't be celibate. There were needs a man had that could not be denied. He had urged Maggie to marry him months ago, but she had steadfastly refused, saying she had to wait until a year after her husband's death. Nor would she consider the intimacies of marriage until after the ceremony.

Morgan Gaunt was a bit puzzled as to why one or another of his enemies, of which he had several, had not spilled the beans to Maggie a long time ago. Maybe, in their way, they had their own code of honor. Or maybe they had kept still because they wanted Morgan to keep still. About their own secrets, which Morgan knew.

There was little, actually, that Morgan did not know about the people of Cottonwood. He patrolled the streets at night. Not for long could a husband visit a woman other than his wife without Morgan knowing it. Nor could a wife slip out to visit another man without Morgan eventually seeing her.

But he kept their secrets and never mentioned his knowledge to any of them. Unless what they did was against the law.

It was dusk when he heard the faint, wild beat of galloping horses, first as a vibration in the ground, then as a growing sound in the hot evening air. He straightened and positioned himself squarely in the middle of the road. His hand touched the grips of his holstered Colt's 45, loosened it slightly and let it drop back into place.

It was a nervous gesture that made him smile faintly to himself. He admitted he was nervous. A lot depended on what happened here in the next few minutes. But he also felt that high exhilaration that always came when he faced a showdown.

He liked his job. He liked the risk of it,

the danger he had to face every day. Now he wondered fleetingly how he would take to a job driving a stagecoach, or a freight wagon, or punching cows out in the lonesome emptiness of the prairie. He shook his head. He didn't know. But he was going to have to find out because this job wouldn't last more than a couple of years at most. Then he'd either have to do something else or move on, to another trail town farther west, and to another after that until finally they all had changed or disappeared.

The thunder of galloping hoofs grew louder. He was briefly grateful that enough light remained for them to see. In complete darkness he'd be overrun before they had a chance to halt.

They saw him, but they came on, maintaining their hard gallop, trying to make him get out of the road. They didn't know him, but they knew who he was because Wedemeier had told them about him.

He neither flinched nor budged. He sat there like a rock, by his own will holding his horse absolutely still. There were at least fifteen riders, too many to count in the poor light and in the dust that rose from their horses' hoofs.

It appeared they were really going to run him down, but at the last instant those in front hauled their horses to sudden, crow-hopping stops, and those behind, of necessity, followed suit.

Gaunt didn't say anything until the horses had partially quieted. Then he said calmly, "Good evening, boys."

None of them seemed to know how to reply. Morgan said, "It's getting dark so you likely didn't see the sign. It says guns are not allowed in Cottonwood. You'll have to check them with me. You can pick them up at the jail on your way out of town."

One man blurted, "Like hell! ain't gettin' my gun away from me."

Another echoed, "Mine neither, by God!" and a third man echoed that.

They spread, now, so that they sat their horses side by side, for the width of the road and for a dozen feet on either side of it. Gaunt knew if he drew his gun they'd riddle him before he got off much more than a couple of shots.

Besides, he didn't want a shoot-out with these men. They weren't criminals and they hadn't broken any law. He said calmly, "Now, boys, you know one man can't shoot it out with fifteen, no matter how good he is. Besides, I don't want to quarrel with you. There's a reason the town don't want men with guns in it. The guns get used. Usually it's some cowboy that gets shot."

Nobody answered him. He said, "The town's waiting for you. The girls. The saloons. The poker games. You'll be treated fairly, and you won't need guns."

"How do we know we'll be treated fairly? That ain't what I heard."

"Then you heard about some other town. You'll get a fair shake here. If you don't, you come to me and I'll personally take care of it." He felt briefly ashamed, promising fair treatment when he knew he couldn't guarantee that was what they'd get. Not in Kurt Vossler's five saloons.

"What if we don't give up our guns?"

Gaunt felt himself go very tense. That tenseness and a reckless disregard of danger both were in his voice when he replied. "Why then I guess we'll just have to shoot it out right here. You'll get me, boys, but I'll get three of you before you do."

He waited, while that sank in. Suddenly the four who faced him abreast in the road began to have second thoughts. A minute passed, then two. Gaunt's arm was tense,

47

so tense it ached, and his hand wasn't more than a couple of inches from the grip of his gun.

Right now it could go either way. Some hothead's nerve might break, and he might yank out his gun. If that happened, nothing could stop it from continuing to its grisly conclusion. Gaunt would be dead, lying in the middle of the road. At least two of the cowboys would be dead, maybe more. And the only thing that would have been settled would be that the drovers could keep their guns in town.

Gaunt's chest began to ache. It was nearly dark now, but there was still enough gray in the sky to clearly see each form. How very much is risked, thought Gaunt, for each small principle. And yet if the risk is not taken, then no principle is upheld.

The tension broke suddenly. One of the four facing Gaunt in the middle of the road said, "Oh hell, boys, we'll get our guns when we leave town. Besides, if it turns out we need 'em, we can always go to the jail and get 'em back."

The dangerous moment was past. Their horses moved, unchecked by the riders. Gaunt's horse began to dance nervously now that the iron hand on the reins had relaxed. He said, "Just buckle the belts again after you take 'em off so I can hang 'em over my saddle horn."

A belt and holstered gun was thrust into his hand, and another, and another after that. The saddle horn wouldn't hold them all so he hung the rest over his head. When he had them all he said, "Go on, boys. You don't need to wait for me. I'm going to be pretty slow with all this hardware hanging around my neck."

That got a nervous laugh out of some of them. They dug spurs into their horses' sides and thundered away over the bridge and into town.

He had won another victory. But it gave him no feeling of triumph. He had promised them they would be safe. It was up to him now to see that they were. If one got hit on the head and rolled, and died because of it, he would have a hard time living with himself afterward or explaining it.

But maybe, he thought, his warning to Vossler earlier would have its effect. Vossler would likely hold back, keeping his places orderly for several days. In a week most of this bunch would be gone. Others would have taken their place.

He rode slowly over the bridge and across the railroad tracks. So heavy were the belts and revolvers that he could hardly dismount in front of the jail. He unlocked the door and went inside. In darkness he removed the belts and holstered revolvers from around his neck. He hung them from the coat tree, just inside the door. He went back out and removed the others from his saddle and carried them inside.

It was time for his evening rounds, after which he would have his supper at Maggie Conover's restaurant.

He locked the jail, mounted his horse and rode slowly up Kansas Street. The names of the saloons were familiar to him, Alamo, Texas, Drovers, Red Dog, Pink Lady, Kansas Pride, Longhorn, Mustang, Bijou, Gold Coin and Overman's. Vossler owned the Red Dog, the Pink Lady, Bijou, Gold Coin and Mustang.

There was a routine to the way Gaunt made his rounds, a routine he knew was dangerous. Except for his early morning rounds, he always started at the same place, took the same route and ended up at the same starting point. He was predictable, but there was something about a regular routine that he liked, even if it was dangerous.

He had told himself often enough that he ought to vary it. Regular rounds made it possible for his enemies to ambush him. But varying his routine was, in his mind, a confession of weakness, an admission of fear. And he'd give nobody the satisfaction of knowing he was afraid.

Already he could hear the high yells of the cowboys coming through the open doors of the saloons. He could hear the tinkle of pianos, the shrill laughter of the saloon girls and, closer, the voices of prostitutes calling out to a couple of the cowboys who were more interested in them than they were in the saloons.

There also was, in Gaunt himself, a fine feeling of tension he always had when the drovers were in town. He grinned wryly to himself, then dismounted at the first saloon he reached, the Pink Lady on the near corner of Kansas and Goliad.

He went inside. This place had attracted most of the cowboys for the simple reason that it was the first one they reached. They lined the bar, each with a girl beside him, each with a bottle in front of him. At tables against the wall, the gamblers waited, idly shuffling cards or playing solitaire.

Gaunt stood inside the door. He had warned Vossler but it wouldn't hurt to warn the gamblers in Vossler's saloons as well. He crossed to the gambling tables and positioned himself with his back to the bar, facing the three gamblers. He said, "Honest games, boys. Three complaints of cheating and out of town you go. Kill anyone, and it will be murder because none of the drovers have got guns."

The three stared at him with sullen anger. None replied. He knew only one of them and had arbitrated two cheating complaints against the man last year. He looked straight and hard at this one. *"One* complaint against you, Moss, and out *you* go. Remember it."

He turned his back and heard Moss muttering as he did. He knew the epithet Moss was calling him, but he'd been called that before, and besides, he knew that if he turned and demanded that Moss repeat it, the man would refuse.

He stepped outside, picked up his horse's reins, mounted and went on to the next saloon. Fewer of the Texans were in this one, still fewer in the next. Those after that were empty, waiting for the Texans who would eventually hit every saloon in town.

Satisfied, finally, that everything was quiet and orderly, he rode his horse up Kansas Street. Now he put the animal up onto the boardwalk and leaned down to try each door. Having done that on one side of the street he crossed over and did the other one. This way he eventually reached the bank.

Main Street marked the end of the business section of town. He rode east to the alley behind the bank, turned into it and began checking the rear door of each establishment.

It was pitch black here. His horse picked his way daintily through refuse and piled-up tin cans. Gaunt's senses were now sharper and more alert because he knew that if and when he was attacked it would probably be in a place like this.

He tried each door all the way down to Alamo Street, then rode along Alamo to the alley between Maple and Kansas Street. He repeated his routine of trying doors all the way to Main and afterward rode back to Kansas Street and along it to its upper end.

Here he turned east, skirted Hooker's hayfields and took the creek bed back to the cattle pens at the lower end of town. He rode through the cattle pens to the railroad depot, rode across the wooden platform and then crossed the tracks and entered Kansas Street again at its lower end.

The entire rounds had taken about forty-five minutes. He continued up Kansas Street, remembering as he crossed Texas Street that he hadn't informed the newly arrived drovers that it was the deadline which they were not to cross. He'd been so busy enforcing the gun ban that he hadn't thought of it.

He reached Maggie Conover's restaurant, dismounted and tied his horse. He went inside.

Most of her customers had already eaten their supper and left. There were only two men sitting at a corner table. Gaunt spoke to them, calling them both by name. Then he sat down at the corner of the counter with a smile at Maggie who had just come through the kitchen door. "Evening, Maggie."

There was a light frown on her forehead. She nodded to him and stood behind the counter facing him. Before he could speak again she said, "Another year." She hesitated and then said, "I worry so. I wish I could stop."

"Nothing to worry about," he said soothingly.

"No? What about that confrontation you had with those cowboys at the edge of town?"

He smiled. "You heard about that?"

"Everybody knows about it. Somebody must have been watching you."

"More than one, I expect."

"You haven't answered me."

"All right. The council passed a ban against guns in town. I had to enforce it. It wasn't hard. I asked them to give me their guns and they did."

"Just like that."

"Just like that."

She put her hands on her hips and looked at him with exasperation. "Morgan Gaunt, you know there was more to it than that!"

"A little," he conceded. "They didn't want to give up their guns. But the next bunch will be easier, and the next still easier. By the end of the season I won't even have to meet them at the edge of town. They'll come to the jail and give up their guns of their own free will."

She was shaking her head now, knowing it was no use arguing the point with him. "What do you want to eat?"

"Surprise me. I like everything you cook."

That brought a faint smile to her mouth. But her eyes were still sparkling, and she was as pretty as he had ever seen her look. She turned and disappeared.

One of the men at the table asked, "Have any trouble getting the guns from those cowboys, Mr. Gaunt?"

Gaunt swung around on the stool. The man who had spoken was Harvey Clay, who owned a hardware store and who was a member of the town council. Gaunt shook his head. "They didn't want a fight. All they wanted was to get to the saloons."

Clay grinned. "You make it sound easy."

"It was."

"You can still have two deputies if you want them."

Gaunt shook his head. "I can handle it."

And he could. Until Vossler hired someone to ambush him in the dark. Until some drunken cowboy challenged him from the middle of the street and began shooting with a gun he'd either hidden or had obtained from someone in town. Until some gambler he had ordered out of town for cheating shot him in the back.

Maggie brought him a plate of roast beef and noodles in gravy and followed that with a steaming cup of black coffee. Hungrily he began to eat.

CHAPTER 5

While he ate, Maggie hurried back and forth between the table and the kitchen at the rear. Whenever she passed, Morgan's glance would raise and touch her. Sometimes she caught his glance and smiled, but once, when she saw a cloud of something that might have been uncertainty in his eyes, she could not force herself to smile.

Morgan was, to her, like a wild thing that has not and cannot be tamed. Like a horse that has run free all of its life and has never known the hand of man.

Could she tame him? She didn't know. Nor was she altogether sure she wanted to. Yet how could she accept life on Morgan's terms? How could she live out each day and night in fear that someone would come knocking on her door to tell her he was dead?

Maybe Morgan could not be tamed. Maybe his destiny was to live violently and die the same way. Maybe she would make a disastrous mistake if she married him.

She caught herself avoiding his glance. Realizing that she was, she stopped directly in front of him and asked, "Do you have everything you need?"

He nodded, his mouth full. Smiling a forced smile, she turned and re-entered the kitchen.

She could not drive away the dark feeling of foreboding that troubled her. It was as if she knew, for certain, that Morgan was going to be killed. She probably shouldn't have been so inflexible about observing a year of mourning before marrying him. She should have agreed when he first asked. If she had, they'd have been married for more than three months by now. She'd have had that much.

But she knew that would not have been enough. Not for her. She wanted a lifetime when she married again. She'd lost one husband and she doubted if she could stand to lose another one.

The two men at the table left and only Morgan Gaunt remained. Maggie cleaned up the dining room, then went into the kitchen and began to wash the stack of dishes piled beside the sink.

Morgan came back, carrying his plate and cup. He slid them into the dishwater, picked up a flour-sack dishtowel and began to dry. She smiled at this unaccustomed touch of domesticity he had assumed, but she could not forget the look of uncertainty she had earlier surprised in his eyes. Was he as unsure as she? Troubled and upset, she finished washing dishes, took off her apron and blew out the lamp.

Morgan followed her out and waited while she locked the door. He untied his horse and walked beside her, leading the animal. Maggie took his arm.

Neither seemed to have much to say, and what they did say came out awkward and strained. At her door, Morgan bent and kissed her on the mouth, holding her briefly but strongly in his arms. He said calmly, "Good night, Maggie," in a voice that, she thought, could as easily say good-bye.

For an instant she clung to him desperately. When she released him he said with surprise, "Well! What was all that about?"

She laughed nervously. "I guess I just can't help being afraid for you."

"No need. I can handle it." His voice held an almost defensive quality.

She knew she should not pursue it, but she couldn't help herself. "Do you intend to continue as marshal, after this year?"

He was silent for a moment. There was a kind of helplessness in his voice when he did reply. "Maggie, I don't know anything else. Except soldiering."

This was not a new subject for discussion between them and Maggie knew she could say nothing she hadn't said before, yet something seemed to be driving her. "Would driving a stagecoach be so dull? Or running a cattle ranch? These Texans don't seem to think it's dull."

His voice was just a little stiff. "We've talked about it, Maggie, and I've said I'll think on it."

"Yes, we have, haven't we?" Her own voice now was cold.

Again Morgan said in his deep, calm voice, "Good night, Maggie."

"Good night." She hated herself for speaking to him in so cold a voice. She hated herself for letting him walk away, a lonely man facing unknown dangers alone, without even letting him know he had her support.

But the sad truth was, she thought as she turned and went into the house, he did not have her support. She hated the job he held. And, she told herself, she wasn't going to marry him unless he agreed to give it up.

As troubled as Maggie, Morgan Gaunt mounted his horse, which he had earlier tied to Maggie's fence, and rode slowly down the middle of the street toward the center of the town.

He had not missed the coldness in Maggie's voice. He was sure now that Maggie was going to make his quitting the marshal's job a condition of her marrying him.

Could he accept such a condition? No, he could not. Not and remain the man he was.

On the other hand, he would have to quit eventually. The life of Cottonwood was limited, probably to no more than another year or two. Whatever trail towns sprang up west of here would also die in time. Which meant he would have to go somewhere else, to another lawman's job that might be as dull as driving stage or running a cattle ranch. So why confront Maggie over this job which he knew he'd have to give up anyway?

He smiled faintly to himself. It was a principle, he supposed. He couldn't let her issue ultimatums to him. He couldn't let her dictate his way of life, at least not that way.

He felt an overpowering sense of loss, as if Maggie already had gone out of his life. He shook himself physically, to throw that feeling off.

It was dark on First Street between Maple and Kansas streets. Dark enough to warn him that preoccupation could, in his line of work, be the death of him. He put Maggie determinedly out of his mind and forced himself to realize where he was, what the situation was in Cottonwood, and what the dangers were. He reached Kansas Street and turned south toward the huge Cattlemen's Hotel.

There were a hundred rooms in the Cattlemen's. At the height of the season, most of them would be occupied because Cottonwood would be full of cattle buyers, railroad men, trail bosses and their *segundos,* who were permitted north of Texas Street, gamblers and maybe a few female singers, who performed in the better saloons, and their managers. There were usually a number of eastern tourists as well, come to see the "wild, wild West."

Gaunt rode down Kansas in the exact center of the street. He stared straight ahead, unwilling to let a constantly roving glance indicate nervousness or fear. Yet his eyes missed nothing on either side of the street and his ears caught every sound.

The bar at the Cattlemen's Hotel and that at the Drovers were both well patronized by men of the town, probably discussing the arrival of the first herd and the confrontation Gaunt had had earlier with the drovers from that herd. He smiled faintly to himself and continued down the street all the way to the jail. This time, anticipating a possible sudden need for the animal, he tied his horse to the cast-iron hitching post in front.

He unlocked the jail door, but he did not light a lamp. Instead, he picked up the straight-backed chair, carried it out and put it down with its back to the front wall of the jail. He sat down and tilted it back against the wall.

For a while, he sat still, letting the sounds of the town be absorbed through his ears, sorting out each sound and identifying it.

So faint was one of those that he could

almost have believed he had imagined it. Yet he knew that he had not and he was moving before it had died away. He hit his horse's back and was off at a gallop in the direction from which it had come. He judged that to be a block off Kansas Street and maybe a couple of blocks uptown.

The sound had been that of a woman's scream, made very faint by distance and by the overriding interference of other sounds. But it had been unmistakable nevertheless to Gaunt's trained ear.

He turned the corner of Kansas and Goliad at a hard gallop, the hoofs of his horse drowning out all other sounds. He whirled onto Oak and now caught a blur of figures up on the corner of Oak and Texas Street. It was so dark he could not distinguish them, but knowing from the scream that a woman was in trouble, he yanked his revolver from its holster and fired twice into the air. On the heels of the second shot's echo, he released a harsh and wordless shout.

He reached the corner, tense and alert, knowing this could be a trap someone had set for him. He left his horse, running, and now, close up, heard the sounds of struggle, a muffled cry, and headed for those sounds.

While he was still twenty or thirty feet away, the woman's attacker broke off and ran. With his hand removed from her mouth, the woman began to weep hysterically. Gaunt reached her and said in his deep, reassuring voice, "It's all right now. He's gone."

She clung to him, slight and small and obviously very young and he stared in the direction her attacker had gone. Voices called questions from the darkness and Gaunt bawled, "Somebody bring a lantern!"

But already he knew the identity of the girl in his arms. Josephina Chavez, waitress at the Drovers Hotel dining room. She lived half a block north of the intersection on Oak. She had been going home.

Men came running, one with a lantern. Josephina's clothing was torn and there was a bruise on her cheekbone, but otherwise she seemed to be all right. Her father, Heraldo, came running and she left Gaunt and ran to his arms.

Someone said, "Those goddamn Texans!"

Gaunt said, "Whoa. She didn't say it was one of them."

"Who else?"

"There's lots of riffraff in town." He touched Josephina's slender shoulder. "Could you tell who it was? A cowboy? Somebody else?"

She was still trembling violently and tried twice before she could speak. She shook her head as she said, "Not a cowboy. Someone whose hands were smooth."

Gaunt was a little surprised that she would have thought of that. To Chavez he said, "She shouldn't come home alone. You should walk with her."

Heraldo's voice was defensive. "And you should keep the streets safe. That's what we pay you for."

Gaunt ignored the criticism. He knew how upset Josephina's father was. They moved away and the crowd dispersed, talking excitedly among themselves. Gaunt mounted his horse and rode back to the jail.

This was one of the prices they had to pay when they tried to run a wide-open town for the Texans. But he was glad Josephina had not been seriously hurt.

He pulled his horse's reins through the ring on the hitching post without tying them so that he could free them easily and resumed his seat in front of the jail. He

fished the Bull Durham sack from his
pocket and rolled himself a smoke, noting
with mild surprise that his fingers were
trembling. Not enough to interfere with
what he was doing, but trembling.

He was that conscious, then, of danger to
himself. Even while he'd been galloping
toward the scream, he had believed in his
heart that it was a trap. He struck a match
and lighted his cigarette, blowing the match
out quickly and dropping it to the walk.

He tilted his chair back comfortably
against the wall. His thoughts turned idle as
he listened again to the muted sounds of the
town, the muffled shouts of revelry, the
women's laughter, the tinkle of a piano
and, up in the Alamo a woman's voice
singing "Oralee."

For the time being he had nothing to do
but listen and remain ready in case trouble
broke out. His thoughts turned to Maggie
and a strange sense of depression came over
him.

It was a sense of loss and yet, he told
himself, he had not lost her. She would
marry him. What if he did have to give up
his marshal's job? He was going to quit it
anyway, if not this year or next then the
year after that.

By insisting on his quitting it, she might, in fact, be saving his life. He smiled ruefully to himself. He was rationalizing, defending her, trying to talk himself into doing something he could not do. He could not permit her to issue an ultimatum to him, even before he married her. Not if their marriage was to succeed.

He thought of Rose with a twinge of guilt. Rose was in love with him. And he was unable to return her love, at least in the way she deserved.

An hour passed. Uptown, all lights except those in the Cattlemen's Hotel and the Drovers, had gone out. The lights in the Alamo cast a soft glow on the walk and out into the street. Men moved back and forth between the various saloons, some walking briskly, some staggering.

Somewhere along Goliad a fight broke out and men's voices shouted angrily. Gaunt rose to his feet and stood there, hesitating. There were no shots and the shouting voices died away. He settled back comfortably in his chair and tilted it once more against the wall.

For a while it was quiet. He thought how unfair it was to disarm the drovers and let saloonkeepers and gamblers keep their guns. At least, though, with the cowboys unarmed there would be little chance either saloonkeeper or gambler would have need to use their guns.

Another hour passed. He came to his feet a second time as a woman's shrilly screeching voice berated some cowboy for something he had or had not done. Again he settled back when the voice had died away.

More herds would probably arrive tomorrow, he thought. Maybe among them that of Buck Robineau. A week from now, Cottonwood would be jam-packed with cowboys and the cattle pens would be full of cattle waiting their turn at the cars.

All through the season new drovers would come, and those whose money was gone would depart. Cottonwood's function was to relieve them all of their money as rapidly and completely as possible.

Gaunt's function was simply to see that the process was orderly.

CHAPTER 6

As the evening wore on, Gaunt occasionally struck a match and glanced at his watch. It still lacked half an hour of being midnight when he finally got to his feet and mounted his horse.

Never before had he begun his midnight rounds so soon, and he wondered why he was doing it tonight. There could be only one reason, but he didn't like to acknowledge it. He was nervous even if he was not afraid. Nervous because of Vossler's threat. Nervous because of the attack on Josephina. Nervous because of the gambler, Moss, in the Pink Lady Saloon, who was perfectly capable of shooting him in the back.

He rode his horse up onto the walk and, leaning down, peered into the Pink Lady Saloon. Moss was sitting at a back corner table, facing toward the door. Gaunt caught

71

the man's eye, his own gaze watchful. Moss's eyes were virulent. Gaunt went on, his horse's hoofs reverberating hollowly.

He crossed the intersection of Kansas and Goliad diagonally, and looked in the door at Overman's, the only saloon west of Kansas Street. Jake Overman was behind the bar. His head was totally bald, his face rough-hewn and coarse. Jake Overman was a hard case, but he'd never given Gaunt any trouble and he didn't keep a gun in the place, saying he was capable of handling anything that happened there. He was, too, thought Gaunt. Overman saw him and raised a hand briefly in greeting. Gaunt acknowledged it, then turned his horse and rode back toward Kansas Street.

He crossed Kansas and rode halfway down the block on Goliad to the Longhorn. Not a single cowboy was in the Longhorn and the bartender was standing in front, smoking a cigar. Gaunt spoke and the bartender acknowledged the greeting with friendliness. Again Gaunt turned his horse and rode back to Kansas Street.

It occurred to him that maybe he'd started his rounds earlier tonight because of the fact that he'd have to return the Texans' guns at two. That might have had something to do with it, of course, but that wasn't all of it. Still, varying the times he made his rounds was smart, and he should have been doing it all along. No use making it any easier for his enemies than it already was.

On Kansas Street he rode up close to the open doors of each saloon and peered inside. He tried the doors of the closed shops and, where there was a padlock, tugged on it to make sure it had been locked properly.

He did not go around into the alleys to try the doors back there. He would do that on his final rounds after he returned the cowboys' guns to them at two. He always liked to check the alleys after the saloons had closed, so he could look for drunken cowboys who might have passed out or for those who might have been slugged and robbed.

That would be the most dangerous time for him and that was the time he feared the most.

His horse's hoofs made a hollow-sounding, comfortable rhythm as he rode slowly along the boardwalk, first on one side of the street then on the other, checking doors. The town council had been talking about putting in concrete sidewalks, but so far they hadn't been able to agree on it.

Maggie's restaurant made him think of her, and he shook off the preoccupation caused by his thoughts. Once more alert, he checked the doors of the bank and then, moving out into the center of the street, headed uptown into the residential section.

Only one light was visible along the length of the street. It was in the parlor window of Bart Chapman's house midway between Second and Third on the west side of Kansas Street. It went out while Gaunt was still a hundred feet away but not before he saw the shadowy figure of a woman slip out the front door. She saw him and ducked behind a huge lilac bush in Chapman's yard.

Morgan Gaunt didn't stop nor did he give any indication that he had seen. But he had seen the woman, and had recognized her too. She was Bessie Overman, wife of Jake Overman who owned Overman's Saloon on Goliad.

Gaunt muttered a curse. Bart Chapman ought to have better sense than to fool around with Bessie Overman. Her husband, Jake, might well be the most dangerous man in town. He'd kill Chapman if he found out, and he'd probably do it with bare hands.

Bessie Overman was already out the front door when she saw the dimly looming figure of the marshal and his horse silhouetted against the saloon and hotel lights farther down Kansas Street. She ducked behind the big lilac bush in Chapman's front yard as the lamp went out and waited for the marshal to pass.

Why was he here so early, she wondered. Never before had he begun his midnight rounds so soon. She and Bart had often timed his passage by the clock. Tonight he was half an hour ahead of time.

He went on by, his horse's hoofbeats muffled by the deep dust in the street. Bessie released a long sigh of relief. Maybe she had not been seen.

Frightened and nervous, she headed toward home, a slight, pretty woman who never got over feeling the guilt of her unfaithfulness. She had been seeing Bart Chapman for almost a year, although she hadn't seen him lately because her husband had not been staying late at the saloon. She tried to justify her unfaithfulness now, as she always did when guilt assailed her, but she did not have much success. Jake might not be an ideal husband and she did not love him; in fact, she never had. But he did support her, he had never struck her despite his violent nature, and when he was not at the saloon he was at home.

Chapman was almost his exact opposite. He was slender and handsome. He had a luxuriant head of hair. He flattered her and made her feel like a desirable woman, something Jake Overman never bothered to do.

But there was no excuse for her infidelity, and she knew that there was not. Yet she also knew she would go on seeing Chapman as long as he wanted her. He knew the risk. He knew how violent her husband was, and he knew Jake could easily break him in two. But he didn't seem to care or else believed they could go on forever without getting caught.

It turned her cold to think that the horseman riding up the street tonight could have been Jake as easily as the marshal. Jake probably would never leave the saloon this early, but he might.

She reached home and with trembling hands unlocked the door. She went inside, almost afraid to light a lamp, almost afraid that when she did she would see Jake standing there, face flushed with rage, eyes accusing her.

Oh God, she thought, I've got to stop. Then she thought of Chapman and of the ecstasy of being in his arms. And she knew she wouldn't stop. She would go on no matter what the consequences might be.

Gaunt rode up the dark street toward Hooker's hayfields at its upper end. Bessie Overman wasn't the only woman in Cottonwood who slipped out at night to visit another man. But Bessie's affair was probably the most explosive because Bessie's husband was so dangerous.

Still, thought Gaunt, there was little he could do about it. All he could do was speak to Chapman and let him know the risk. If Chapman and Bessie then chose to go on, there would be nothing further he could do.

He had always liked Bessie Overman. And he liked Chapman well enough. But he also knew Chapman was a ladies' man who would discard Bessie as soon as another woman caught his eye. Chapman probably deserved what happened to him, if anything did. But Bessie did not. Gaunt smiled at his own inconsistency. His sympathies were with Bessie. Had he been a woman, his sympathies would probably have been with Chapman instead.

The truth was, if his sympathy was anywhere, it ought to be with Overman.

He reached the upper end of town where all the houses were dark, skirted Hooker's fragrant hayfields and then rode his horse down into the bed of the creek. An animal, spooked by the horse, bounded away. A deer. He tensed briefly at the noise and then relaxed. He was jumpy, all right. Too jumpy for this early in the year.

The ban on guns was partially responsible. So was the confrontation earlier today. But maybe, he thought, he was also getting tired. And weariness was a luxury he could not afford.

It was peaceful riding in the pitch-black bed of the creek and there was little chance anyone would try to ambush him here. Shooting was too risky when there was no light at all.

He climbed his horse out of the creek bed at the lower end of town and picked his way down the alleyway between the cattle pens after first opening a creosoted gate. It was utterly still, and what smell there was consisted mostly of the creosote with which the gates and planks had been treated and the dust-dry manure lying deep inside the pens.

He was loose and relaxed now but he had the feeling that his hearing had never been sharper nor his eyesight more acute. He reached the end of the pens, opened and closed another gate without dismounting from his horse, and headed for the depot, looming darker against the sky.

A single square of light was visible at this end of the depot. Gaunt rode his horse up onto the platform. His hoofbeats sounded thunderously against the thick planks.

Vague uneasiness touched Gaunt as he came into the square of light being thrown through the window and onto the platform. For just an instant he felt like a target. He had to force himself to stop his horse, bend down in his usual leisurely way and tap on the glass as a greeting to Jim Sutton, the telegrapher.

Sutton, who had glanced up as Gaunt's horse stepped onto the platform, returned the greeting and Gaunt went on, letting his breath sigh out inaudibly as he was swallowed by the darkness again.

His own jumpiness bothered him. Was it,

he wondered, a hunch or premonition that something was going to happen to him? Or was it simply that he'd been on this job one too many years and should have quit before the cattle shipping season began? He didn't know.

What he did know was that he hadn't quit, and the town couldn't get another marshal this late in the year. He had to stay.

He entered the lower end of Kansas Street and halted at the jail. Without dismounting, he listened for a moment to the jumbled sounds of revelry. Easily then he swung from his horse and passed the ends of the reins through the ring on the hitching post.

His chair still sat on the sidewalk in front of the jail. He sat down, hitched at his gun so that it would be available, then tilted the chair back against the wall.

He fished his sack of makings from his vest pocket and rolled himself a smoke. The match made a glowing spot of light against the pitch-black bulk of the jail.

He felt more relaxed than he had all day. He supposed he had settled his doubts and had fatalistically accepted all the risks a few moments before when he realized it was too late for the town to get another marshal, that it was therefore impossible for him to quit. And that was a definite relief to him. Now perhaps he could quit worrying and simply do his job.

He finished the cigarette and ground it out beneath his heel. Like a statue he sat, watching, waiting, listening.

Once, nearly an hour after arriving back at the jail, he struck a match and glanced at his watch. It was half past one. In another half hour the saloons would begin to close and shortly after that the cowboys from Wedemeier's herd would come by for their guns. After that he'd make his final rounds, checking to see that all saloons had closed and that all doors to the town's business establishments were secure.

CHAPTER 7

At about a quarter past two, the first of the drovers arrived at the jail to pick up their guns. There were three of them, all drunk enough to stagger. Owlishly they picked through the weapons hung on the coat tree and identified their own. Gaunt passed them out and the cowboys mounted and rode out of town.

Another group arrived, to repeat the procedure, and another after that. Finally, at two-thirty, only three guns remained.

Two more drunken drovers arrived shortly afterward, one of these obviously very angry about something, the other trying to quiet him. Sullenly the pair accepted their guns, mounted and rode south toward the railroad tracks. Which left Gaunt with one gun and cartridge belt. He stared at it for several moments, then went outside and peered into the darkness up Kansas Street. No lights visible except for the dim night lights at the Cattlemen's and Drovers hotels.

Gaunt felt a stir of uneasiness. He wondered where the missing cowboy was. He hoped he wasn't lying dead behind one of the saloons, his pockets turned inside out. It was much more likely, of course, that the Texan was either passed out someplace or was spending the night with one of the girls. He'd check that out when he made his rounds.

He waited another ten minutes in the silent darkness. Then he mounted his horse and rode up Kansas Street to begin his final rounds.

At Goliad he turned left and rode as far as Overman's, which was dark and silent. He checked the door and found it locked. Leaving, he thought about Bessie Overman and Bart Chapman, and briefly felt sorry for Jake Overman. He returned along Goliad, checked the Longhorn on the other side of Kansas Street and also found it locked.

He returned to Kansas Street and checked the door of the Pink Lady Saloon where the gambler, Moss, made his headquarters. It was dark inside and the door was locked. That shouldn't have increased his nervousness, but it did.

Now he turned up Kansas Street, checking each saloon he passed. All were dark. All their doors were locked, with one exception. The Red Dog. Sully had apparently taken longer to close than the others had. As Gaunt drew abreast, he stepped from the door, accompanied by another man, then turned and snapped the padlock shut.

Gaunt was about to speak, when a shout came from across the street. "All right, you cheatin' sonsabitches, let's see if you're as tough out here as you are in your goddamn saloon!"

Gaunt froze, himself less than a dozen yards from the pair. There wasn't enough light for accurate shooting, only a small amount from the stars, but the cowboy might possibly score a lucky hit. The chances of either Sully or the man with him hitting the cowboy were slimmer, at least until they had a muzzle flash at which to shoot.

But Gaunt had no intention of letting it go that far. To Sully and the man with him, he said, "If either of you is armed, keep your heads. There's damn little chance he can hit anything with no more light than he's got. I'll take care of it."

Sully said sourly, "Then take care of it."

Gaunt asked, "What's his beef, anyway? You cheat him?"

"No cheating. He lost his money, is all. I never saw a heavy loser yet that didn't claim he was cheated."

Gaunt didn't believe Sully, but this was no time to argue it. He turned his horse and slowly paced him across the street toward the place from which the cowboy's voice had come. He called, "All right now, son, don't do anything you're going to be sorry for."

The cowboy squawled excitedly, "Marshal, you just stay out of this. That goddamn gambler cheated me and the bartender backed him up. Threw me out of the saloon. Nobody does that to me and gets away with it!"

Gaunt guessed it must have happened while he was at the other end of town making his rounds. The cowboy had probably gone to one of the other saloons, borrowed some money from one of his friends and kept drinking until all the places closed.

It angered him that a thing like this could have happened the first night the cowboys were in town. He'd warned Sully and Vossler, but apparently his warning hadn't done much good.

In a calm and measured voice he said, "Son, I'll see that you get your money back. I don't allow cheating in this town. You should have come to me and let me look into it."

Sully bawled, "Damn you, if you give him his money back it's goin' to be out of your own pocket. He wasn't cheated. He just lost."

Gaunt turned his head and his voice was like a whip. "Shut your mouth, Sully! Don't open it again!"

He was now halfway across the street. He kept trying to see the cowboy, but it was too dark. There was a passageway over there between two buildings maybe a couple of feet wide and Gaunt supposed that was where the cowboy was.

He said softly, "Son, I don't know who you are. You pull back out of that passageway and skedaddle back to your herd and nothing will be done about this. I'll send your gun out with one of the bunch that comes to town tomorrow."

There was no reply. Gaunt said, "Son . . ."

Suddenly a voice from the passageway yelled excitedly, "Marshal, you stay out of this! I got no quarrel with you, only with that cheatin' pair of bastards across the street."

Until now, Gaunt had supposed the cowboy was the one who failed to pick up his gun at the jail. Now he realized this was the angry one who, with his friend, had picked his gun up last. The one who hadn't picked his up was still unaccounted for.

He had stopped his horse, just short of the edge of the boardwalk. He was listening, for a scuffing sound, for the sounds of the cowboy's breathing.

His horse fidgeted. Suddenly the animal looked toward the passageway. His ears pricked forward.

The cowboy was still there. Gaunt said, "Son, I'm coming over there. You got nothing against me, and you don't want to shoot me. You fade back out of that passageway and I'll see that you get your money back tomorrow. You got my word on it."

He touched his horse's sides with his heels and the animal stepped forward. Gaunt meant to ride right to the passageway and block it with his horse's bulk. He didn't think the cowboy would shoot.

But the horse had taken no more than two steps when the cowboy's voice bawled, "Oh no you don't!" Flame blossomed from his extended gun, once, twice.

The first bullet went wild. The second raked a burning gouge along Gaunt's left thigh. And suddenly he was no longer a controlled and thinking man. Instinct took over. His hand went like lightning to his side. His gun came out of its holster in a blur of motion, the hammer back and the gun ready to fire before he ever leveled it.

The cowboy fired again, this bullet going past Gaunt's right ear like an angry bee. After that Gaunt didn't hesitate. He fired, slightly left of the cowboy's muzzle flash and a few inches higher.

Gaunt was diving from his horse before his own muzzle flash had died away. He hit the deep dust of the street on both feet but his left leg folded because of the bullet wound and dumped him in the dirt. The cowboy's gun was silent now.

Cursing soundlessly at the leg that had let him fall, Gaunt struggled to his feet. Gun in hand, he limped painfully toward the passageway.

He was almost sick at his stomach because he knew what he was going to find. He reached the passageway, nearly falling over the yielding, prone body of the cowboy. He knelt, put his hand on the cowboy's chest, then took it away. The man was dead.

For an instant his fury knew no bounds. Sully and his crooked gambler had succeeded in getting him to do their killing for them. He wondered bleakly what else he could have done, and knew he'd had no other alternative. It had been his job to prevent a shoot-out between the cowboy and the two across the street. He had done what he was supposed to do. It just hadn't turned out the way it should.

He knelt there, numb with shock. He'd seen many dead men. He'd killed several men himself. But he never stopped experiencing that strangely bleak sense of loss, of something precious destroyed that can never be replaced.

With forlorn hope, he put his hand on the cowboy's chest again, praying silently to himself there would be movement there that he had missed before. But there was not.

He got slowly to his feet, his weight off

his wounded leg which now was burning fiercely with the pain. Blood had soaked his pants; it had run down his leg and into his boot. He could hear voices now, uptown, an indistinct murmuring of question upon question. What's going on, they wanted to know. What's happening?

He turned his head and stared at the dark front of the Red Dog across the street. He could now see the two blurred, indistinct shapes of Sully and his gambler. He would run them out of town, he thought, not doubting for an instant that they had, indeed, cheated the cowboy and then thrown him out of the saloon.

Suddenly, unexpectedly, muzzle flashes blossomed across the street. A bullet took out a window not two feet from Gaunt's head and shards of broken glass showered to the walk. Others thudded into the wooden facades of the two buildings.

Gaunt dived for the passageway, stumbling over the cowboy's body and sprawling full length inside the passageway. He was faced away from his attackers and it was awkward turning around. He did it, though, and then shoved his revolver out in front of him, resting his arm on the body of the dead cowboy.

He understood instantly the way Sully and his gambler friend were thinking. Shots had been fired, supposedly at them, by the cowboy who had challenged them. No one would blame them for shooting back. And if the marshal happened to be in the way, if the marshal happened to get killed . . . Well hell, this end of town would probably want to give them a medal, and the other end of town probably wouldn't object too much. He was necessary as all policemen were, and people acknowledged that. But down deep they didn't really like him or approve of him.

He could have killed Sully and the man with him. He could see both of them dimly against the lighter wall of the saloon. But he held his fire, lying still, knowing that in a few minutes the street would be swarming with townspeople and neither Sully nor the man with him would dare continue shooting at him.

Besides that, he had killed once tonight and he would not kill again. Not so soon. Not if there was any other way.

The voices up the street were coming closer now. There was a lantern, bobbing along, throwing flickering light on the buildings on both sides of the street.

And from the cribs farther downtown and over on Maple and Oak came the voices of the girls, asking each other what was going on, and who had fired all the shots.

Gaunt finally got to his feet. Absently he punched the empties out of his gun and replaced them with live ammunition from his belt. His horse, made nervous by the shots, had moved away downstreet and now stood fifty feet away.

The man with the lantern reached Sully and the gambler, standing in front of the Red Dog Saloon. Gaunt knew they couldn't shoot him now. He crossed the street, slowly, limping on his wounded leg.

The man with the lantern asked, "What's going on? What's all the shooting about?"

Gaunt did not reply. He was looking at Sully and the gambler. He swung a hand and the flat of it struck Sully on the cheek with enough force to snap his head aside. The bartender made a move toward his gun, and Gaunt rammed a fist into his belly, a blow that made Sully double and go white with pain.

Gaunt relieved both Sully and the gambler of their guns. He said, "You've got until sundown tomorrow to get out of town. If I see either of you after that, I'll shoot on sight. Is that understood?''

Maybe they had expected him to charge them with trying to kill him a few moments before and had prepared their defenses only for that. Neither man offered any protest or defense.

Only their eyes threatened him. Both men turned and walked away.

By now a crowd of perhaps a dozen men had gathered in front of the Red Dog Saloon. A couple had wandered across the street and were looking down at the still body of the cowboy lying on the walk.

Gaunt said, ''Somebody get Ira Blanton down here to pick up the body.''

A man hurried away. Gaunt looked up Kansas Street and saw Rose Navarro standing in front of the Alamo, a wrapper clutched around her, looking worriedly downstreet. Maggie Conover was nowhere in sight.

He walked up the street to where Rose was standing, trying not to limp. She said, ''You're hurt,'' her face white with shock.

''Not much. A crease.''

''You could have been killed.''

It was true, but he couldn't admit it to himself or to her. He said, ''I'll be all right.''

"You'll let the doctor look at it?"

"Yes. I'm sorry I worry you."

She forced herself to smile. She knew if he could walk, he was not too badly hurt. She turned and went back into the Alamo and climbed the stairs to her room.

Damn! damn! damn! she thought. Why do I have to fall in love with a man who walks the streets making a target of himself? Why do I have to play second fiddle to a woman who hasn't even the sense to take what is offered her?

She slammed the door furiously. She felt tears burning behind her eyes. I won't cry, she thought. Damn it, I won't!

But she did. She threw herself on the bed with sobs already wracking her. She wept until she was exhausted and could weep no more.

He was a fool, waiting for Maggie Conover to finish her year of mourning and consent to marry him. He was a fool, letting Maggie Conover dictate to him how he would earn his living and how he would work.

But she was the biggest fool of all. For asking nothing of him. For giving everything she had to give.

She got up and went to the window. She

stared down into the street. There were several lanterns down there now. She could see Morgan Gaunt, not bothering now to hide his limp.

She had thought all her tears were gone. But they were not. They filled her eyes again as she stared down at him.

He had been lucky tonight. But he was doomed. Before the last of the Texas cattle were shipped East, Morgan Gaunt would be dead.

CHAPTER 8

Maggie Conover did hear the shots. Already awake, worrying and wondering what she ought to do, she flinched at the first and flinched again at each succeeding shot. She threw back the covers and sat up on the edge of the bed.

Three shots. She hurried into the parlor and stepped out onto the porch in her nightgown and bare feet. She couldn't see or hear anything.

What did three shots mean? That someone had tried to kill Morgan, certainly. And probably that he had fired back.

Three shots instead of one or two was encouraging, she knew. Morgan Gaunt was probably all right. One shot would almost certainly have meant that he was dead. Suddenly there was another flurry of shots. Again she flinched at each.

She could feel violent tremors beginning in her knees. She sat down like a child on the top porch step and hugged her knees to stop their trembling. She couldn't stand this, she told herself desperately, not any more. She couldn't stand lying awake night after night worrying. She'd tell him to-morrow. She'd tell him that she'd marry him immediately but only if he would give up the marshal's job. She'd tell him that if he didn't, they were through.

There were no more shots. What if he was dead? That second burst of shots had not been reassuring.

She knew she couldn't stand not knowing whether he was all right or not. She wouldn't sleep a wink if she didn't find out for sure. She got up and hurried into the house. She put on slippers and a wrapper, then went out, crossed Maple and hurried along Second to Kansas Street.

Down at its lower end lanterns were moving around like fireflies. The figures of milling men were visible, and she strained her eyes trying to pick out Morgan Gaunt.

She saw his horse. A few moments later she saw a man's figure that must certainly be his. The man was limping painfully.

Her breath sighed out softly with relief.

He was alive, then. Only hurt. One of the bullets must have struck him in the leg.

For an instant she felt deep compassion for his wound, his pain. Then she said fiercely to herself, "I'm glad he's hurt! I'm glad! Now maybe he'll be sensible. Maybe he'll give up this job."

A few others had heard the shots and had come into the street or onto their porches to stare downtown. Conscious of their glances, Maggie hurried back toward home. She reached her house, went in and locked the door.

She stumbled back to her bedroom, removed her wrapper and threw herself onto the bed. For several moments she lay there trembling.

The tears came like a flood. She sobbed hysterically for a long, long time. She felt helpless and alone because she didn't think Morgan would do what she wanted him to do, and because she knew she would break off with him if he did not.

It was more than two hours before she finally could sleep.

It must have been nearly half an hour before Ira Blanton's black hearse came down the street drawn by a team of bays.

When the hearse was used at funerals it was always drawn by two teams of gleaming blacks, but for picking up a body, a single team was used. Ira made a turn in the middle of the street and pulled to a halt in front of the passageway where the cowboy's body lay.

Gaunt and Ira lifted the body onto a canvas that Ira had laid in the hearse to protect the interior.

Blanton was a short, stubby man who was enormously strong in spite of his rotund appearance. He whistled. "Hell to pay, huh?"

Gaunt said, "I'm afraid so."

"I suppose you want me to wait for word from the trail boss about the funeral."

"That's right. I'll ride out first thing in the morning and tell him."

"Who killed him, Sully or that gambler?"

Gaunt realized he didn't even know the gambler's name. He said, "Neither. I did."

Blanton whistled again. But he didn't comment. He went around and climbed to the driver's seat. He drove away, heading for his furniture store and undertaking establishment on the south side of Main behind the bank.

Gaunt was conscious not only of the pain in his leg but of the blood still flowing from the wound. His foot squished inside his boot with every step he took. He walked to his horse and picked up the reins. To the crowd he said, "That's all. Go home and go to bed."

Still worried about the cowboy who had not picked up his gun, he mounted and rode uptown toward Doc Kelley's house on Third and Oak.

There was a light in the parlor and another in the adjoining room that served as Doc's examining and operating room. The door opened before Gaunt could dismount and Doc stood framed in it, crowned by a halo of bushy white hair. Gaunt limped up the walk and Doc said, "The shots woke me up. I figured someone would need patching up."

He stood aside and Gaunt went in. Gaunt went straight into the examining room. He stuck his left boot into the boot jack on the floor and pulled it off. His face turned white with pain. He left a bloody footprint on the floor when he put down his bootless foot.

Doc said impatiently, "I could have got that off."

"Sure. With a knife. That's a damn good pair of boots." He was already pulling the other off. Sweat stood out in beads on his forehead from the pain.

"Don't want me to cut your pants either, I suppose."

"Why cut them? I can get them off." He already had them off. In his long, bloody underwear he sat down on the table's edge.

Sarcastically Kelley asked, "Is it all right if I cut your underwear?"

Gaunt shrugged. "Go ahead."

Doc Kelley pushed him back and Gaunt was glad to lie full length. His head was reeling and his leg was burning savagely. He felt Doc working at cutting his underwear away from the wound. He closed his eyes.

In a calm and steady voice Doc kept him posted as to what he was doing and what he thought. He said, "Deep. Ragged too. But it didn't get an artery, and it didn't touch a bone. Son, you've lost a hell of a lot of blood. You're going to feel woozy for a day or two. Ought to stay in bed, but I don't suppose it's any use to tell you that."

He poured something on the wound to disinfect it, something that made blackness come down like a curtain over Gaunt's consciousness. Then he laid a thick compress over the wound and began to bandage it. "I'm not going to stitch you up because that will draw the wound together and make it pull. This way it'll leave a bigger scar, but it won't pull and it won't keep you from moving around."

He finished bandaging. By then Gaunt's head was clear again. He sat up and reached for his pants. Doc carried the bloody boot out back to rinse the blood out of it. When he returned he was drying the inside with a towel. He handed it to Gaunt, who put it on.

Gaunt got to his feet. His pants were very tight over the bandage. He asked, "How much, Doc?"

"A dollar."

Gaunt gave him a dollar. "Thanks. I'd better go back to the hotel and change clothes. Then I've got to make my rounds."

"Any chance of you getting shot again? If not, I'll go back to bed."

Gaunt grinned. "No chance. Go back to bed," knowing he lied even as he spoke.

Already he was in trouble with Wedemeier and his drovers over the cowboy's death. If anything had happened to the other missing cowboy there would be hell to pay. In any case, he had to know. He had to find the man.

He went out, limped to his horse and mounted. In front of the Drovers Hotel, he drew his horse to a halt. He swung down, limped to the tie rail and looped his reins around it. He went in, nodded to Hughie Jordan, the night clerk, then crossed the tile-floored lobby to the stairs.

Climbing them hurt, but he did his best not to limp. He reached his room, unlocked the door and went in. Groping, he found the lamp, struck a match and lighted it.

He found clean underwear, pants, socks and shirt, and with a bit of pain in his wounded leg, he changed his clothes. He then belted his revolver around his middle, withdrew the gun and checked the loads. Reloading was automatic with him after he had fired his gun, but he was taking no chances that he might have forgotten it.

He blew out the lamp, went out and locked the door behind him. It wasn't that he had anything he thought might be stolen. He was being careful. He didn't want to walk into a dark room and find someone waiting there for him.

Pain and the loss of so much blood had weakened him. He clumped downstairs, favoring his leg, and went out onto darkened Kansas Street. Mounting his horse, he rode slowly down Kansas to the jail, staying in the middle of the street, his senses painfully alert. He heard no sound, saw nothing move. The brothels all were dark, the girls asleep.

He rode back to Goliad and turned right toward the Longhorn. When he came to the alley, he turned into it, holding his horse to a slow walk. He knew he'd never see the missing cowboy in this complete darkness. He would have to count on his horse to reveal the man's presence, either dead or unconscious but alive.

Now, as sightless as if he were blind, he watched his horse's head and ears. He rode all the way to Texas Street, then turned and retraced his steps, this time trying each rear door as he did. The route was familiar to him; he knew each shed, each sagging fence, each pile of tin cans and trash.

He was still about a hundred feet from the alley mouth when his horse's head turned suddenly to the right. The horse's ears pricked forward nervously.

Gaunt wasted no time. He left the saddle with a single, swift movement, hitting the ground first on his good leg, afterward bracing himself with the wounded one.

Made nervous either by his rider's nervousness or by what he'd seen, the horse danced away. Gaunt's gun was in his hand, the hammer back, while he tried to pierce the darkness and see what his horse had seen.

Nothing moved. No sound broke the silence. The hairs on the back of Gaunt's neck were erect, the flesh crawling underneath.

How long he stood there motionless he didn't know. But when nothing happened, he moved forward, a careful step at a time, as alert and ready as he had ever been in his life.

Three steps. Four. He was out of the alley now, passing a sagging stable at the rear of the Kansas Pride Saloon. Suddenly his boot encountered something soft and yielding and he stopped, knowing what it was, praying silently to himself that the cowboy wasn't dead. He knelt, still alert, still not looking down. This would be the perfect place for Sully and his friend to ambush him, because he would be busy with the prostrate cowboy and not expecting it. But nothing happened. No guns roared. There was no sound.

He put his hand on the cowboy's chest,

almost weak with relief when he found it rising and falling regularly. And now the sour smell of whiskey reached his nostrils, the drunken cowboy's breath.

He picked up a stick and threw it against the building wall, knowing this sudden sound would startle anyone who might be waiting in the darkness for a chance to shoot him down. But still no sound came. Still nothing moved.

Satisfied at last, Gaunt lowered the hammer on his gun and shoved it into its holster at his side. He pushed his hands under the cowboy's body and lifted it. He carried it into the alley to his horse.

With a soft grunt, he heaved it up and over the saddle. Then, leading the horse with one hand and steadying the cowboy with the other, he continued north along the alley to Texas Street.

The Drovers Hotel was on the corner of Kansas and Texas streets. He looped his horse's reins around the rail, slid the cowboy's body off the saddle and onto his shoulder, then carried it into the lobby of the hotel.

Hughie was asleep. Gaunt struck the bell and Hughie came awake with a start. Gaunt said, "A room for him."

"Yes, sir!" Hughie grabbed a key and came around. He crossed the lobby, hurrying, with Gaunt right behind.

Climbing the stairs made sweat beads spring out on Gaunt's forehead, but he made it to the top without having his leg give way. He carried the unconscious cowboy along the hall to the door Hughie had unlocked for him. Hughie was inside, lighting the lamp.

Gaunt dumped the cowboy on the bed. Hughie asked in a scared voice, "Is he all right?"

"He will be tomorrow. Except for a headache. Tell him to stop at the jail for his gun on his way out of town."

Gaunt bent and went through the cowboy's pockets. There was some money, a pocket knife, a few extra cartridges for his gun. Gaunt blew out the lamp. He said, "Leave the key here so he can get out in the morning. But lock the door from the outside."

"Yes, sir." Hughie obeyed, closing and locking the door from the outside with his master key. He followed Gaunt downstairs.

At the desk, Gaunt asked him for an envelope. He counted the money and wrote the amount on the outside of the envelope.

He sealed it and handed it to the clerk. "Give it to him when he comes down in the morning."

"Yes, sir." Hughie put the envelope underneath the counter top.

Gaunt went out, conscious of a vast relief. He still had to explain the other cowboy's death, but at least this one was all right.

He untied his horse and mounted to continue his final rounds. His leg was bleeding again; he had opened it carrying the drunken cowboy upstairs. The bandage on it was soaked, and the blood had seeped through and stained his pants.

He wished tonight's rounds were over with. It would feel good to lie down and close his eyes.

CHAPTER 9

Up Kansas Street he rode. He thought about Bessie Overman when he passed Bart Chapman's house. He went on, troubled by his thoughts, hoping Bessie would discontinue her relationship with Chapman before her husband found out about it. Cottonwood was no different than any small town—its inhabitants liked to gossip. If he knew about Bessie's relationship with Chapman, it was certain other people also did. And they would talk.

Farther up the street, where he would normally have turned to go to Maggie's house, he wondered if she had heard the shots earlier. When she knew he'd been wounded tonight she was certain to renew her demands that he quit the marshal's job. And he didn't know how to answer her. He didn't want to break off with her. Just the

109

thought of losing her made the future bleak.

On he went, finally reaching the upper end of town where Hooker's hayfield was. He skirted it along the barbed wire fence and, when he reached the brushy bed of Cottonwood Creek, rode his horse down into it.

It was darker here because of a diminished light from the stars. It was hard to see anything, even for Gaunt, whose eyes were accustomed to the dark. But his horse seemed to have no trouble avoiding obstacles.

He let the reins go slack, contenting himself, in the absence of vision, with listening. He heard the katydids, the soft murmur of the creek, the scurrying of field mice and other small rodents. Once he startled something larger, a deer probably, and the animal bounded away, crashing through the brush.

He watched his horse's head, knowing if there was a man or men waiting for him to pass, the horse would smell or see them a long time before he did. But the horse plodded along, never raising his head, never pricking his ears.

He reached the lower end of town and climbed his horse out of the creek bottom at the railroad bridge. From here he rode to the cattle pens, still empty, and picked his way along the main alley separating them. Now, even more than before, he kept his glance on his horse's head, sure that the horse would spot anyone a long time before he did.

But nothing happened. He reached the end of the cattle pens, opened the gate and let himself out, closing it behind him, all without leaving his horse. The gate squeaked thunderously as it closed.

That ought to wake them up, he thought, and he could feel himself growing even more tense than he had been before. Only a small distance now separated him from the jail.

He reached the depot. A square of light showed the location of the telegraph office. The sound of his horse's hoofs on the wooden platform as the animal jumped up onto it made Jim Sutton, who had been asleep, raise his head. Gaunt's every nerve was tense as he rode past the window, briefly silhouetted against the square of light.

The report, though expected, startled both Gaunt and his horse. It came crashing out of the darkness, preceded by the barest split second by the muzzle flash. Gaunt's horse jumped a foot into the air and three feet ahead and Gaunt knew he had, at least, been stung by the bullet.

With no urging from his rider, the horse thundered briefly along the wooden station platform, leaving it with a long, running leap. For all of that short distance two guns a dozen yards away flared and racketed, the bullets tearing holes in the frame walls and windows of the station and showering splinters and broken glass onto the platform below.

Gaunt, keeping his seat easily despite the horse's terror-stricken flight, placed the shots before the horse leaped from the platform. There was a pile of ties a dozen yards to the right, and the two gunmen were hidden behind the ties.

Immediately he reined the horse hard to the right. He dug his heels into the already frightened horse's sides, urging him to even greater speed, heading him straight for the pile of ties.

In the dim starlight, he saw two figures materialize from the dark bulk of the ties. They sprinted away toward the cattle pens. Jim Sutton had come out onto the railroad platform and now he yelled querulously

112

into the darkness, "What the hell's going on?"

The frantic speed of the fleeing gunmen was no match for the running speed of Gaunt's horse. The animal overtook the first man and tried to swerve to avoid striking him. Gaunt wouldn't let him swerve. The horse's chest struck the man, knocking him end over end.

The horse tried to slow, now, but Gaunt would not permit it. His heels drummed against the horse's sides and the barrel of his gun flayed the horse's rump.

Seconds after striking the first man, he drew abreast of the second. Half a dozen feet separated them. Gaunt reined the horse aside, forcing him right up against the running man.

His gun barrel descended, striking the man's head with a sodden sound. The man disappeared.

Only now did Gaunt haul the horse to a halt and turn him, once more digging in his heels. The horse leaped forward. Gaunt knew the second man was out of it. He also knew the first could still be dangerous.

And he was right. Flame blossomed ahead of him and a bullet went by a couple of feet away, humming like a bee. The gun's report cut off the sound.

Once more the horse ran straight into the man, who turned to flee when he saw he was going to be run down again. Too late. The horse struck him and knocked him flying for a second time.

This time Gaunt left the horse in mid-stride. Trained to do so, the horse came to an instant halt when he felt Gaunt leave the saddle. Gaunt's wounded leg collapsed under him as he touched the ground and he fell, rolling in the dust. When he came to hands and knees, the man who had shot at him was less than ten feet away—raising his gun.

Gaunt said sharply, "Don't! Don't or you're dead!" The man dropped his gun.

Gaunt pushed himself to his feet. He was angry now with a cold, harsh anger he seldom felt. He walked to the man and, reaching down, seized his coat collar and yanked him to his feet. The man struggled and cursed and Gaunt, out of patience and hurting now, clipped him on the side of the head with the barrel of his gun. The man sagged and Gaunt let him fall.

Over on the station platform, Jim Sutton called, "Marshal? You all right?"

Gaunt called back, "I'm all right." He

went to his horse and took the rope down from its place beside the saddle horn. He made a loop and stooping, put it around the unconscious man beneath his arms. Straightening, he walked to the other man, stooped and dragged him back. He made the loop large enough to go around both men beneath the arms.

Holding the end of the rope, he went to his horse and mounted, trying to favor his wounded leg, which was still bleeding. He looped the rope around the saddle horn.

He drummed on the horse's sides with his heels. The rope came taut and the horse moved away, turning sideways, prancing because of the strange burden dragging along behind. Gaunt's hand on the reins was firm.

The dust was deep and a cloud of it raised behind the two dragging men. One of them came to and yelled with protest but Gaunt neither answered nor stopped.

Across the railroad tracks he went, with the two men bumping over them and on beyond to Kansas Street and from there straight to the jail, a total distance of a block and a half. His horse maintained a steady walk.

He rode beyond the jail so that the pair

he was dragging would stop immediately before the door. Then he threw the rope off the saddle horn and dismounted with it in his hand.

One of the men, the conscious one, tried to throw off the loop so that he could rise. Gaunt pulled back. The man failed to get enough slack to free himself.

He reached the pair. Both men were of approximately the same build so he could not distinguish between them. Besides, both were covered thickly with dust.

One was struggling. Before Gaunt realized what he was doing, he yanked a derringer from some hidden place, leveled and fired it.

So angry was the man and so much in a hurry that the bullet went wild. He never got a chance for another shot. Gaunt's foot lashed out, struck his forearm with enough force to make him shout with pain. The derringer dropped into the dust and Gaunt picked it up.

He stooped, his leg afire with pain now. He yanked the men to their feet, one by one. Both were conscious, although one was very unsteady on his feet. Gaunt said harshly, "Into the jail."

They were slow to move so he put a hand on the back of each and gave a shove. Both men staggered toward the door of the jail.

Gaunt followed. The jail door was locked so they could not go in. He said harshly, "Put your hands in the air and keep them there."

They complied. Swiftly Gaunt searched them for hidden weapons, being very meticulous and thorough about it because he knew carelessness could and would cost him his life. Satisfied that neither had another gun, he unlocked the door and pushed them roughly inside.

Both staggered all the way across the room. Gaunt found the lamp and lit it. Now, in the light, he could tell the men apart. Both Sully and the gambler glared at him murderously. He said, "Back to one of the cells. Go on!"

They turned and shuffled into the corridor between the two rows of cells. Gaunt said, "Inside. Move!"

They stepped into one of the cells. Gaunt closed the door behind them and locked it with his key.

He could feel himself go limp now that the danger was past. He looked at the gambler. "What's your name?"

"Jackson."

Gaunt nodded, turned and went back to

the office, closing the separating door behind.

He blew out the lamp and went out the door. Mounting, he rode his horse to the livery barn. The animal hadn't worked up a sweat since this morning, so there was no need to rub him down now. Gaunt led him to his stall and got him a measure of oats and a couple of generous forks of hay. He patted the horse's neck, briefly examined the bullet crease on the horse's rump and then went back out into the street.

He returned to the jail, glad his horse hadn't been hurt more seriously. The shallow gouge he had sustained would heal in a week or so.

Inside the jail again, he lighted the lamp. He sat down, tilted his chair back and put his feet up on the desk.

With Sully and Jackson in jail, he knew he didn't dare go to the hotel tonight. But it wouldn't be the first time he had slept on the office cot.

He found the makings in his pocket and rolled himself a smoke. He lighted it, feeling himself relax now that the long day was done.

Tomorrow he had to ride out to Wede-meier's herd and try to explain the cowboy's death to Wedemeier and to his men. He knew what he would say. "He tried to kill me and I had no choice." They'd have to accept it. They had no other choice. But he didn't like the explanation any more than they would. There ought to be a better way to settle things.

His leg ached ferociously. Blood had soaked all the way through the bandage and there was a spot of it on his pants as big as his hand. He eased the leg to the floor, trying to get it into a position where the pain would ease.

But the pain did not diminish no matter how he moved the leg. He'd play hell sleeping tonight, he thought.

Glancing at the clock, he saw that it was already three-thirty in the morning. He opened a desk drawer and took out a bottle and a glass. He dumped the glass half full of whiskey and gulped it down. He poured the glass half full a second time.

His thoughts began to wander now. He thought of Rose, and a small smile touched the corners of his mouth. He thought of Maggie, and the smile disappeared. He thought of Bessie Overman, and a slight frown touched his face.

His thoughts returned to Wedemeier. He

hoped the trail boss would be satisfied to let his dead cowboy be buried quietly. But he doubted it. Wedemeier's cold neutrality only masked an underlying hostility. Wedemeier had heard about Marshal Gaunt and had believed everything he'd heard.

And if more herds arrived tomorrow, as was probable, Gaunt's job was going to be complicated even more. He found himself hoping fervently that one herd, at least, would not arrive until all this had quieted. He hoped that Buck Robineau would not arrive for another week.

CHAPTER 10

Gaunt was drowsy now, both from weariness and the whiskey he had consumed. He got up and headed for the office cot. He sat down on it and with difficulty because of his wound, pulled off his boots. He got up and was about to blow out the lamp when he heard a knock on the office door.

Glancing that way, he saw Rose Navarro standing in front of it. He crossed the room, trying not to limp but not succeeding very well, and opened the door.

He stood aside and Rose came in. She threw one hasty glance at his face, which he supposed was pale and drawn with weariness. Then she looked down at his leg, at his blood-soaked pants. She glanced up at his face again.

Her own face was pale, without makeup, and her eyes were filled with compassion

121

for his pain. "Thank God you're alive at least! I heard all those shots, and I had to know!"

She was clad in a nightgown with a wrapper over it. She had slippers on her feet. He said, "Sully and a gambler named Jackson tried to get me down by the depot. I've got them in jail."

There was a touch of exasperation in her expression and he knew what she was thinking. But she didn't voice her thoughts. Instead she asked, "You're not going to bed with that leg bleeding the way it is are you?"

"It'll stop as soon as I quit moving around on it."

"It should be dressed again. That bandage will be stiff as a board by morning when it's dry."

"It'll be all right."

She faced him, hands on hips. "It will not be all right! You just come with me to the doctor's house or else I'll get him to come down here!"

He stared at her pale and angry face. She was not a woman to make demands, but she sure was making one now. And he knew she'd do exactly what she said she would. He shrugged. "All right. It don't look like it's much use arguing with you."

"It's not."

He sat down on the cot again and pulled on his boots. He tried not to show how much it hurt but he could feel the sweat breaking out in beads on his forehead. When he stood, she took his arm, to steady him.

He left the lamp burning, but he locked the door when he went out. Together they walked slowly along the street, Rose trying to support his wounded side but not succeeding very well. He tried not to limp.

Doc's house was nearly seven blocks from the jail. In front of the Alamo, Rose said, "I should have gotten a buggy. Or asked Doc Kelley to come to the jail."

"It's all right," he said, and it was. He liked her close beside him and he liked the faint perfume that rose from her hair. It hurt every time he put his left foot down, but it would have hurt almost as bad lying on the cot at the jail.

Rose said, "You said it happened down by the depot. Were they waiting for you there?"

"Uh-huh. Tried for me as I crossed in front of the telegrapher's window."

"You're lucky."

"I suppose I am."

"What about tomorrow? How are you going to tell that trail boss that you killed one of his men?"

"Show him what his man did to me, I guess."

The town seemed to be asleep. No lamps showed anywhere. Gaunt was drenched with perspiration when they reached Doc Kelley's house. Rose helped him to the door and Gaunt knocked on it.

A lamp was lighted somewhere in the house. It got brighter as it was carried to the front door. The door opened and Doc asked, a trifle irritably, "You shot again?"

Rose answered for him. "He needs his leg wound dressed. It's been bleeding badly."

Rose stayed in the parlor while Doc took Gaunt into his examining room. Doc closed the door and Gaunt used the boot jack to pull off his boots. He dropped his pants. "There goes another suit of underwear."

Doc was already cutting it away. "Maybe I ought to have sewed that wound up. You've lost a hell of a lot of blood. How much do you think a man can spare?"

"Didn't you sawbones used to bleed a person for just about everything that went wrong with them?''

"*I* didn't!" Doc's face got red, and then he grinned at his own anger. He unwound the bandages as gently as he could. The compress, beneath the bandages, had been stuck to the wound but all the fresh bleeding had loosened it and it came off easily.

Gaunt stared at the raw and ugly wound, even now seeping blood. Doc prepared a fresh compress, saying as he did, "You got to be more careful. Can't you stay off of it?"

Gaunt looked wryly at him. "What do *you* think, Doc? There's one herd here already and a man dead that I've got to explain. There will probably be two or three more herds arriving tomorrow."

"All right. All right. Forget I mentioned it. But you take better care of yourself or you'll be flat on your back and Cottonwood won't have *any* law."

He finished bandaging and Gaunt stood and pulled up his pants. Getting his boots on was no easier than it had been before, but he managed it. He paid Doc and went back into the parlor where Rose was waiting, nervously pacing back and forth. She looked worriedly at Doc. "Is he all right?''

Doc shrugged. ''Needs to stay off that leg. But he won't. He as much as told me he wouldn't. Maybe you can get him to use his head.''

She smiled faintly. ''He's a stubborn man.''

All Gaunt wanted now was to get back to the jail and get to sleep. Besides, he was beginning to worry about Sully and Jackson. They undoubtedly had a lot of friends, some of whom might try to break them out of jail if they knew it was unguarded.

He said, ''Let's go, Rose.'' Turning, he looked at Doc. ''Thanks. Sorry we woke you up.''

''Any time. Don't let it worry you. Nobody ever gets shot in the middle of the day.''

He followed Rose out into the street. The lamp went out behind them before they had gone a hundred yards.

Gaunt laid his arm across Rose's shoulders, using her for support. This way, they went over to Kansas Street and along it toward the jail at the lower end of town.

Rose didn't speak and neither did Gaunt. He tried to find a way to put his weight down on the wounded leg that would hurt it least but nothing really seemed to help.

At the Alamo, he stopped. "I'll be all right now. Thanks for—" he hesitated an instant and finally finished—"worrying about me."

"You'll get some sleep now, won't you?"

"Uh-huh."

She stood on tiptoe to kiss him. "Good night."

"Good night, Rose." He waited while she unlocked the door of the Alamo and went inside. He waited until he heard it lock behind her and then hobbled on down the street toward the jail. He knew it must be after four o'clock. He wasn't going to get much sleep, but even a few hours would help.

Limping slowly along the walk, he thought of Rose. It seemed strange to him that it had been Rose, not Maggie, who had worried enough about the shots to come see if he was all right. Strange too that Rose, not Maggie, had worried enough to insist that he go to Doc Kelley's and have his wound freshly dressed.

Always before he had kept the two women in their proper perspective. He loved them both, but differently. He needed Rose and she fulfilled his need, giving him, he had often thought with shame, much more than he gave her.

But in his way he needed Maggie too. Not so much for now but for the future. They would raise a family and live and grow old together. Hard as it would be, he would leave Rose forever when he married Maggie, and he knew Rose understood this as well as he.

It would not be easy for her any more than it would for him. He reached the jail, unlocked the door and went inside quietly, not wanting to awaken either Jackson or Sully and have them yelling at him.

He locked the door behind him. He did not light a lamp. He stumbled across the room, found the boot jack by feeling for it with one foot, and pulled off his boots. He stumbled to the cot and laid down on it.

His leg throbbed mercilessly, but the bandage did not feel wet to his touch so he knew that the wound had not bled enough for the blood to soak clear through.

His head whirled. He had the sensation that the cot was turning over. He thought of what faced him tomorrow.

The first thing he'd do would be to release Sully and Jackson. He'd repeat his order and give them until sundown to get out of town.

After that he'd ride out to Wedemeier's herd and tell the boss about the cowboy that he'd killed. He dreaded that. He knew it would be difficult.

He caught himself wondering if the cowboy would still be alive if he'd handled the incident differently. Maybe he shouldn't have tried to put himself and his horse between the cowboy and the two men he was trying to kill. Maybe he should have tried to get Sully and Jackson to retreat back into the saloon and given the cowboy time to reconsider. Maybe if he'd promised the cowboy that he'd not only get his money back but would run Sully and Jackson out of town . . .

He shook his head wearily. Second guessing wasn't going to help. He'd done what he'd thought was best, taking the direct approach that was so characteristic of him. He shouldn't blame himself because the outcome had been tragic and unfortunate.

Determinedly, he tried to sleep but it eluded him. He knew he faced an eventual showdown with Maggie, who had demanded and would continue to demand that he quit the marshal's job. And he couldn't do it. Not in mid-season when the town needed him the most. The only way he could even consider it would be if he was able to find a replacement he thought could handle the job. Which was next to impossible.

He wondered if she would break with him when he refused. She hadn't exactly said she would, but he knew she had come close to it. But maybe when the chips were down she wouldn't break off with him at all.

Then he remembered her face, the firm line of her jaw, her steady eyes. And he felt depressed again.

Finally, as the first faint streak of gray was forming above the eastern horizon, he went to sleep.

Rose Navarro was not so lucky. She lay awake until long after the sky turned light, after the sun came up.

She knew she was a fool, to care so much for him. The trouble was, fool or not, she couldn't help herself.

There was a way, of course, to get him away from Maggie Conover. Let Maggie find out about her and about the relationship she enjoyed with Gaunt. But she couldn't do it. She possessed an extraordinarily strong sense of honor that would not even permit her to consider it.

She buried her face in her pillow and wept. Why, she asked herself, hadn't she met him a long time ago? Why hadn't she been stronger, and found a way to support herself without going into a saloon?

She thought of Maggie Conover. She wanted to hate Maggie, but she could not. The truth was, she both liked and admired Maggie Conover, and she knew Maggie would be a good wife to him—if he survived this season, which at the moment did not seem too likely.

Tomorrow he would have to ride out and tell that trail boss and his crew that he had shot and killed one of their friends. And even if he survived that all right, there were other herds coming. In two weeks there would be fifty to a hundred thousand cattle waiting their turn at the loading chutes.

And there was Robineau, a bitter man who had been brooding since last year, who had threatened to return this year and kill Gaunt. Robineau couldn't face Gaunt in a fair fight, crippled as he was. So he'd shoot from ambush, use a shotgun, or get Gaunt in a crossfire from which there could be no escape.

It seemed to Rose that Morgan Gaunt was doomed. And when he died, she might as well die too.

CHAPTER 11

It was half past eight before the yelling of Morgan Gaunt's prisoners awakened him. Sunlight was warm in the street outside the jail. He swung his legs over the side of the cot and sat up. His wounded leg still ached, but it was better than it had been last night.

He remembered instantly all that had happened yesterday. He pulled on his boots and stood up. He walked to the door leading to the cells, opened it and asked, "What the hell are you two yelling about?"

Sully asked, "What about some food?"

"I'll get it." He closed the door, ran his fingers through his hair, belted his gun around his waist and settled his hat upon his head. He opened the outside door, stepped out into the street and, turning, locked the door.

The air was warm but pleasant. There

was a slight north wind, and it carried the smell of fresh-cut hay from Hooker's hayfields at the upper end of town. A few people were moving in the street. Gaunt headed for the Drovers Hotel, trying not to limp. He didn't want anybody getting the idea that he wasn't able to carry out his duties as usual.

He climbed the veranda steps and went in. He nodded at the clerk behind the desk, then crossed to the stairs and climbed them to the first floor. He unlocked his room and went inside.

It seemed like days since he had awakened here yesterday. With a spare smile at the thought, he took off his vest and shirt and poured some water into the white china basin. He washed, then lathered his face and, while the lather softened his whiskers, stropped his razor. He began to shave.

Finished, he dried his face and stared at himself in the mirror, looking for some clue as to why he so stubbornly held onto his marshal's job. What he saw was what he had seen every day for as long as he could recall; calm, steady eyes, a mouth that was wide and firm, hollow cheeks and high cheekbones, possibly the heritage of some Indian forbear, and a chin that jutted out.

He put on a clean shirt, shrugged into his vest and settled his hat on his damp, freshly combed hair. He went out, locked the door and descended the stairs.

Josephina Chavez was the only waitress working in the dining room. He ordered breakfast and asked that she prepare two trays for his prisoners. He rolled himself a wheat-straw cigarette and puffed it with enjoyment.

He was not alone in the dining room. Over in the corner was a large table occupied by the mayor, Lester Ives, and several members of the town council. They stared at him and, when he glanced back, looked away almost guiltily. They had obviously been discussing him.

He was sure their discussion had not been critical. But they were worried.

He nodded at Ives, who immediately got up and came to his table. Ives said, "Good morning, Mr. Gaunt."

"Good morning."

"We . . . when you finish your breakfast would you mind coming over? We'd like to talk to you."

"All right."

Ives hesitated a moment and then returned to the others. Josephina brought

Gaunt's breakfast. He was hungry and the food made him feel better even if it didn't relieve the aching in his leg. Finished, he got up and strode to the corner table, limping slightly but not too noticeably. He pulled out an empty chair and sat down, nodding to Sam Kohn, Bart Chapman, Dave Ryan and Harvey Clay. "Good morning, gentlemen."

"Good morning, Mr. Gaunt."

"What can I do for you?"

There was a moment's hesitation as each man looked to the other, not having decided on a spokesman. Finally Lester Ives said, "We're worried, Mr. Gaunt."

Gaunt grinned. "So am I. I've got to ride out to Wedemeier's herd this morning and explain that cowboy's death."

"How's your leg?"

"Sore. But it isn't going to incapacitate me, if that's what you mean."

Ives looked relieved. "We're not being critical, Mr. Gaunt. You had no choice last night when that cowboy shot you. But there's no way we can get another man to take your place. Not this late in the year."

Gaunt grinned faintly. He said, "Maggie?"

Ives smiled nervously. "It's pretty well

136

known that she wants you to quit. And with you wounded, we thought . . ." He stopped.

Gaunt said, "I won't quit you in the middle of the season, gentlemen. Unless I'm killed or incapacitated."

All of the men looked relieved. Ives said, "If there's any way we can help . . . deputies . . . anything."

"Thanks. I can handle it."

The conversation was at an end. Gaunt got up and returned to his table. Ives and the others left. After several minutes, Josephina brought the two trays. Gaunt paid for his own meal, signed the check for the other two and left the dining room with them.

The mayor and the council members were standing on the veranda, lighting up cigars and pipes and talking. Gaunt looked at Chapman. "Mind helping me with these trays, Mr. Chapman?"

Chapman looked surprised, but the others didn't seem to notice it. Gaunt handed one of the covered trays to Chapman and accompanied him off the veranda and across the street. He waited until they were well out of earshot and then he said, "I saw Mrs. Overman leaving your place last night."

Chapman's face darkened. He started to say something, probably that it was none of Gaunt's business, but Gaunt was ahead of him. "It's none of my business, of course. But I know Jake Overman. He's a man of violent temper. He'll kill you if he finds out."

Chapman's face had lost much of its color. Suddenly it was almost gray. Gaunt said, "And he will find out. No matter how careful you are, he will eventually find out."

"You haven't told anyone . . . ?"

"Of course not! And I won't."

Chapman's face mirrored his relief. They reached the jail and Gaunt unlocked the door. He carried in his tray and put it on the desk. He took the other from Chapman's hands, who excused himself hurriedly and left. Gaunt smiled humorlessly, wondering why people always thought they were too clever to get caught. But he had Chapman thinking differently. Chapman knew if Gaunt could catch Bessie leaving his house, her husband could too.

Gaunt carried the trays back and gave them to Sully and Jackson. Both men sat down on their cots and began to eat. Their clothes were still dusty from having been dragged. They were unshaven and dirty, but Gaunt didn't offer them the opportunity to wash. He was going to release them soon and they could get cleaned up then.

He went back out into the street and walked to the stable to get his horse. He saddled and bridled the animal, checked the already healing bullet crease, then rode down the inclined plank ramp to the street. He turned to the jail, dismounted and tied his horse to the hitching post, which was still in the shade. He went inside.

Sully and Jackson had finished eating. Both men stared at him suspiciously as he unlocked their cells. Sully asked, "What the hell are you doing?"

"Turning you loose."

The suspicion in Sully's eyes increased. He said, "Yeah. And you'll shoot us down as we leave and claim we tried to escape."

"You know me better than that." Gaunt's eyes were like ice.

"Then why . . . ?"

"I don't want to fool with you. I haven't got time for two-bit badmen. Get out of here and be out of town by sundown. If I see you after that, I'll shoot on sight. And don't come back. Ever."

Sully said, "Damn you . . ." but he cut what he had been going to say short when his eyes met those of Gaunt. He shuffled along the corridor, through the office and out the front door. On the walk in front of the jail he looked back. Gaunt was bringing the trays out so that he could return them to the hotel. Sully said, "Let's go," and the pair hurried up Kansas Street. They turned on Texas and disappeared.

Gaunt carried the two trays back to the Drovers Hotel. Then he returned, untied his horse, mounted and began his morning rounds.

As he passed Maggie Conover's restaurant, she came to the door and stared at him. He stopped, touched the brim of his hat. "Good morning, Maggie."

Her face was cold. "I heard more shots last night after I went to bed. Were they fired at you?"

He nodded.

"Who? Another of those Texas cowboys?"

He shook his head. "A saloonman and a gambler."

Her face was paler as she said, "And you were lucky again."

He nodded. "I was lucky again." Her

coldness bothered him, but he didn't know what to say to change it.

She turned and went back inside the restaurant without speaking to him again. He went on, frowning slightly. It was hard not to compare Maggie's attitude with that of Rose. Rose's worry for his safety took the form of compassion and freely offered help. Maggie's worry only seemed to make her cold and hostile toward him.

He rode up Kansas Street, nodding or speaking frequently to passers-by. The morning air was cool and fresh, and he paused for several moments at the fence that surrounded Hooker's hayfield, breathing in the pleasant fragrance of fresh-cut hay. Hooker had turned a few horses in on the hay stubble and they were grazing quietly in the middle of the field.

Reluctantly, Gaunt went on. He was late making his rounds this morning, and he still had to go out to Wedemeier's herd.

In spite of that, he took his time riding along the bed of Cottonwood Creek, listening to the meadowlarks and wondering what it would be like, owning and operating a ranch. With Maggie. A light frown touched his face. He wondered, in spite of himself, if Maggie would try controlling him in other ways from time to time, wondering too how he would react to her when she did.

Angrily, he put those thoughts out of his head. He touched his horse's sides with his heels and the animal broke into a lope. He felt disloyal and guilty for having had any doubts about Maggie.

The cattle pens were still empty but he knew they wouldn't stay empty long. Already a solitary engine was backing cars along the track to position them in front of the cattle chutes, arranged so that three cars could be loaded at one time.

Wedemeier's herd would have started at daybreak and would be halfway here by now.

His horse stepped up onto the station platform. This morning, Jim Sutton came out onto the platform, blinking against the glare which was not entirely cut by his green eyeshade. He asked, "You all right?"

Gaunt grinned. "Those two are lousy shots."

"I picked up a couple of guns this morning. You want them now?"

"All right."

Sutton went into the telegrapher's office and returned, carrying two guns. He passed them up to Gaunt, who unloaded both into his hand, then passed one of the saddle strings through both trigger guards and tied them on his saddle.

Sutton asked, "What you going to do with those two who shot at you?"

"I turned them loose. Told 'em to be out of town by sundown."

"Think they'll leave?" Sutton was looking at him worriedly.

"They'll leave."

"What if they try killing you again?"

"In daylight? They're not that kind. They'll leave."

He rode to the end of the platform and his horse stepped down into the dust. He crossed the tracks at the intersection, which the puffing engine had now vacated, and rode to the jail. He dismounted, untied the two guns and carried them inside.

One belt and gun still hung from the coat tree. He frowned at it, then took it down and carried it outside. He locked the office door.

He mounted and rode uptown to the Drovers Hotel where he had left the drunken cowboy last night. He went in and left the cowboy's gun at the desk, with instructions to give it to the Texan if he was on his way out of town. He didn't know where the cowboy's horse was, but since he hadn't seen it tied anyplace, he supposed one of the man's friends had stabled it.

He realized he was dreading the confrontation with Wedemeier and had been delaying his departure from town. The realization irritated him enough to make him mount immediately and head out of town at a steady trot. Maybe it *was* time he quit this job. He'd never postponed dangerous or unpleasant things before.

CHAPTER 12

Gaunt held his horse to a steady trot. The animal was fresh and wanted to run, but Gaunt held him in. He didn't want sweat on the horse when he reached Wedemeier's herd. He didn't want them thinking he had come in haste because they were sure to draw conclusions if they did.

Grass lay dry and golden in the morning sun. Meadowlarks trilled their melodious song, but today Gaunt didn't hear. His face wore a frown. However he justified his killing of the cowboy last night to others, he couldn't justify it to himself. He should have been able to stay his hand. He shouldn't have acted automatically, without thought.

Wryly he thought that if he had not acted automatically, he would probably be the dead one this morning instead of the cowboy.

145

A mile from town, he saw dust on the road ahead and a little later was able to make out the figure of a galloping horseman. Squinting against the morning glare, he finally identified Leon Satterfield.

The boy reached him and pulled his horse to a plunging halt. He was excited as he cried, "Marshal! There's two more herds bedded down south of here. I talked to the men. They said there was another right behind that will get in sometime today. Know whose it is?"

Gaunt smiled grimly. He knew whose herd it was, but he wouldn't deprive Leon of the pleasure of telling him. He asked, "Whose?"

"Buck Robineau's, that's whose! What you going to do about him, Mr. Gaunt?"

"Can't do anything, Leon, until he breaks the law."

"But he swore he'd come back this year and kill you, Mr. Gaunt!"

Gaunt's smile widened. "If he does, *then* he'll have broken the law and I can arrest him."

Leon didn't see the grim humor of that. He said, "Mr. Gaunt, it ain't going to be no fair fight. He'll likely use a shotgun on you."

"Don't worry about it, Leon. A year's a long time. Maybe he's changed his mind." He remembered Robineau now, whip slender and wiry, with a broad, sweeping mustache that dominated his face and eyes above it that were so blue they were the things you remembered about him when all else had faded from your mind.

The hell of it was, he'd probably have liked Robineau, even been friends with him had the circumstances been different. Just as he'd probably have liked the cowboy he'd killed last night if he'd had the chance.

Leon was looking at him expectantly. Gaunt fished in his pocket and brought out fifty cents. He tossed it to the boy who caught it expertly. "Thanks, Mr. Gaunt."

Gaunt acknowledged the thanks with a nod. They rode on at a brisk trot for a couple more miles, until they could plainly see the dust of Wedemeier's herd ahead.

By the end of the summer, this lush grassland would look like bare ground, Gaunt thought. The Texas herds that came late would have to bed as much as fifteen miles from town in order to find feed. But the grass always came back no matter how badly it was overgrazed.

He wondered what changes the next five

years would bring. The cattle would stop coming, at least to Cottonwood. They'd go someplace else west of here, maybe to Dodge City when the railroad had reached that far. This grass would lie golden and unused unless somebody filed on it and bought cattle to graze on it.

He suddenly looked at the land with different eyes. He could be one of those who claimed this rich grassland. He could file on a quarter section, and Maggie could file on another one. That would give them half a section, and whenever adjoining land was put up for sale they could buy. Hell, they might wind up with a damn fine ranch. He grinned faintly to himself. The excitement of the marshal's job would be missing but maybe living with Maggie would be excitement enough. She had a temper and pretty definite ideas about how a man ought to conduct himself. Life with her sure wasn't going to be dull.

Wedemeier's herd drew closer until individual animals were visible behind the point rider. Most of the herd was hidden by a cloud of dust.

Gaunt and Leon left the road and angled to the left. Point rider and the lead steers plodded past. Gaunt could see two flank riders and farther back, the remuda, being driven by a single man.

Wedemeier must have seen Gaunt through the dust because he came galloping toward him, accompanied by two of his men. They hauled their horses to a plunging halt a couple of dozen feet away. Wedemeier's eyes were red from the irritation of the dust and possibly from sleeplessness. He asked harshly, "Well, what happened to Jordan and Livingston?"

This was the time Gaunt had dreaded. He said, "I don't know which is which, but one of them passed out in an alley and I took him to the Drovers Hotel and put him to bed. He'll probably be along pretty soon."

"What about the other one?" Wedemeier's eyes were slitted and suspicious.

"He's dead."

"Dead?" Wedemeier's eyes were accusing even before he heard Gaunt's explanation.

"I killed him." Gaunt moved his horse so that the trail boss could see the large spot of dried blood on his pants. "He was trying to kill a bartender and a gambler he claimed had cheated him. I tried to calm him down. Promised him his money back. I promised him that if he'd back away, the whole thing would be forgotten. But he must have been too drunk. Shot me and I had no choice.''

''You told them they'd be safe without their guns.''

Gaunt had been hoping for this remark. ''He'd have been safe without his gun. The trouble was, he made out like he was leaving town, and I gave him back his gun. Then he came back.''

Wedemeier was scowling angrily and so were the two men with him. Wedemeier asked, ''What about the two men that cheated him?''

''I ordered them out of town. They've got until sundown tonight.'' He didn't mention that Sully and Jackson had tried to kill him last night because he knew if he did Wedemeier would want to know why they weren't dead too. It was a question he didn't want to have to answer, because the answer wouldn't have satisfied even him.

The truth was, they were alive only because their bullets had missed. He hadn't stopped thinking during that attack because he had not been hurt. In the cowboy's case, the wound, its shock and pain, had made his instincts take over from his mind.

Wedemeier said, ''By God, we won't give up our guns today.''

Gaunt said, ''Yes you will. Or you'll

tangle with me. I'd advise you, if you want to avoid any more trouble, to tell your men to give up their guns peacefully. Otherwise somebody else is going to get killed."

"Yeah. You."

"Don't count on it. I'm pretty hard to kill."

"Know who's half a day down the trail?"

"I know."

Wedemeier stared at him with grim satisfaction. "Maybe I'll tell my boys to leave you for him."

Gaunt nodded. "That will be fine." He heard hoofbeats on the road behind him and turned his head. The cowboy he had put to bed at the Drovers last night was coming at a lope. Wedemeier said, "That's Livingston. So it's Jordan you killed."

"His body is at the undertaker's. If he didn't have any money left, the county will bury him."

"Like hell. We'll bury him." Without another word, Wedemeier turned and rode back toward the herd. The two cowboys followed him.

Gaunt and Leon rode on, with Leon staying half a length behind. The boy asked, "Lord, Mr. Gaunt, what you gonna do?"

Gaunt looked back at him. "It's all right,

Leon. Lots of men say things they don't mean when they're all stirred up.''

"Where you goin' now?"

"I'll ride out to those two herds that just arrived and tell 'em no guns are allowed in town. Want to go along and show me where they are?"

"Sure, Mr. Gaunt. I oughta do something to earn that fifty cents."

"All right then. You take the lead."

Leon kicked his horse and moved into the lead. Gaunt was tired from lack of sleep last night. His eyelids felt heavy. He let his horse plod unguided behind Leon's, the reins slack. He let his head sag onto his chest. He closed his eyes.

He dozed in spite of his worry about how things were going to turn out. He could only do his best, and he was damned if he was going to let worry about various possibilities turn him into a nervous wreck.

Hearing Leon's call he opened his eyes and raised his head. In the distance, he could see the lift of dust. Leon turned his head and said, "There's one of 'em, Mr. Gaunt."

Gaunt nodded. They went on, with the herd and riders gradually materializing out of the dust and distance. To avoid spooking the herd, Gaunt turned off to one side and Leon followed him. The pair sat their horses on a knoll while the herd went slowly past. As the drag drew abreast, a couple of men detached themselves and trotted their horses toward them.

Except for the gun ban there would be no need to meet each newly arrived herd. Yet Gaunt felt no criticism toward the council for having passed the ban. It would save lives in the end if he was successful in enforcing it. It might even save his own life.

In addition, it would mean that bullets would not be continuously flying through the air with the chance that any one of them might find an innocent target, a woman or a child.

This trail boss was burly and grossly fat, seeming too big for the horse he rode. Instead of riding in the stirrups like most men did, this one rode in the saddle, like a lump of clay, sticking to it even while the horse was at a trot as if his pants were glued to it.

Folds of flesh nearly hid his eyes, which reminded Gaunt briefly of the eyes of a huge, fat boar. Gaunt said, "Howdy. I'm Gaunt, marshal of Cottonwood."

The man's expression did not change. The expression of the cowboy behind him was neutral, showing nothing at all. He said, "Heard of you."

"I don't know what you heard, but regardless, you and your men will be treated fairly in Cottonwood. If anybody gets cheated at cards, come to me and I'll take care of it. If anybody gets too drunk and ends up with his pockets turned inside out, come to me and I'll see that he gets his money back."

"Why don't you just clean up your dirty town instead?"

A bit of steel touched Gaunt's narrowed eyes. "Because you boys don't want a clean town. You want women and gambling and all the liquor you can drink. All I can do is straighten things out when they go wrong."

For several moments the two men stared at each other. Finally Gaunt said, "I didn't get your name."

"Rosen. Used to be Rosenstock, but I shortened it."

Gaunt reached out his hand and Rosen took it reluctantly. Gaunt said, "One other thing. The council has passed a ban on guns inside the town. You and your men will check them at the jail as you ride in.

It's just beyond the depot on the right hand side."

"Oh no you don't. You'll never get the guns away from my boys!"

Gaunt stared at him a moment. The eyes of the two men locked, and held for what seemed an eternity. Rosen's horse suddenly fidgeted and this gave the man an excuse to let his glance slide away from Gaunt's. Gaunt said, "Your boys are coming in for some fun, not to fight. Tell 'em that. If I see a man wearing a gun in town, it's either give it up or fight."

Rosen studied him for a moment more. Finally he shrugged and turned his horse away. He trotted back toward his herd.

Leon asked excitedly, "What if none of 'em turn in their guns, Mr. Gaunt? What will you do then?"

"They'll turn 'em in. Don't worry about it, Leon."

"But what if they don't?"

"They'll turn 'em in." Gaunt couldn't think beyond that. If one herd got by without turning in their guns, then none of the drovers would. And if none of the drovers did, Gaunt's life wouldn't be worth a dime. The only way he could keep the lid on things was by maintaining strict control.

He had a fleeting doubt that he would be able to keep the lid on things. Wedemeier's crew would be coming in tonight, angered by the death of their friend. Getting them to give up their guns a second time was not going to be an easy thing.

And the men from this herd and the other, farther back . . . they would only surrender their guns if Wedemeier's men already had.

It boiled down to enforcing compliance from the first drovers to hit town. Today, those would be Wedemeier's. He touched his horse's sides with his heels and rode on, with Leon leading the way to the second herd.

He delivered the same message to a trail boss named Harkness, whose reaction was much the same as Rosen's. Then he said good-bye to Leon and headed back toward town.

Half a mile from town, he passed Wedemeier's herd. He went on, knowing he would have to wait to demand the drovers' guns until after they had corraled their herd, loaded the waiting cars, and ridden into town to celebrate the completion of the drive.

CHAPTER 13

When Gaunt reached the depot, he stepped his horse up onto the platform. Jim Sutton had come out of his telegrapher's office and was watching the Wedemeier herd as it moved into the pens. Looking back toward town, Gaunt saw that people were clustered at every vantage point, also watching. The arrival of the first herd of the year was an event. They watched from rooftops, from second-story windows, from the crotches of trees and, if they could find nothing higher, from the beds of wagons and buckboards. A bunch of boys came running and jumped up onto the station platform to watch beside Gaunt's tall horse.

The pens had wide, flaring wings pointing toward the south. Into this opening rode the point rider, followed by the lead steers of the herd. The corral wings were wide enough so that the cattle weren't spooked until they were well inside, and by then it was too late. Inexorable pressure from behind kept them from stopping or turning no matter how frightened they became or how much they wanted to go back.

Wedemeier's cowboys kept pressure against the drag of the herd. Up front, responsibility now belonged to the workers in the cattle pens. Mounted on short, powerful mustangs, they opened and shut gates, expertly filling this pen and then the next, until Wedemeier's herd had disappeared and had become instead of a single herd only groups of bawling steers, confined in the various pens.

It always gave Gaunt pleasure to watch this operation because it was so efficient and precise. Gates opened and cattle streamed into the desired pens. When the gates closed, the stream went on to the next pen and the next. No matter how these wild Texas steers bawled or fought, or tried to run, they were helpless, hemmed in by their own kind and by the stout pens, made to go this way or that by the opening and closing gates and by the yelling men on horseback who moved among them.

On the railroad siding the switch engine

puffed and hissed, and the cars waited at the chutes with their doors open.

Where the wide wings of fence that had funneled the herd into the pens narrowed down, men sat on the top rail, with pads of paper and pencils, tallying. When the last animal had entered the pens, they climbed down and walked to windward, where the dust was less, and climbing to the top rail sat side by side and compared their totals. Wedemeier was with them, listening, occasionally commenting.

Wedemeier knew how many cattle he'd had when he left Texas. He knew approximately how many he had lost on the trail. Wedemeier wasn't going to quibble about a few animals. But he wanted the tally to be reasonably correct.

He apparently was satisfied. He accepted a draft from Bart Chapman, climbed down, gathered his cowboys around him and headed toward the foot of Kansas Street.

Gaunt could feel the tension rising inside of him. Now was the time he had to confront Wedemeier and his crew. Now he had to enforce the gun ban again. He smiled grimly. It hadn't been easy last time, and it would now be no easier. One of Wedemeier's crew had been killed. Never mind that he'd had his gun returned and had then gone back into town to use it against the marshal and get himself killed for his pains.

He touched his horse's sides with his heels and the animal stepped down off the platform into the dust. Wedemeier and his men were coming along an alley between the cattle pens. The tension, the strain, the responsibility of the long drive was over and the release was visible in them even at a distance of a hundred yards.

Gaunt's mind was like an animal in a trap, racing back and forth from one possibility to another, frantically seeking some solution, some way out of this that would not result in a shoot-out in front of everyone in town.

He was outnumbered. He could neither outdraw all of Wedemeier's men, nor could he survive if the guns came out. There was a good chance that five minutes from now he'd be lying lifeless in the dust while Wedemeier and his crew rode on, the men to draw their pay at the bank and then go to the saloons for the beginning of a real rip-snorting spree.

He wondered briefly if either Rose or Maggie was watching. He hoped neither was, but that chance was slight. Both were probably watching, wondering how he was going to get out of this alive. They knew he couldn't let Wedemeier and his crew enter carrying their guns. Nor could they see how he could get the cowboys' guns away from them. Not after one of their number had been killed by him last night.

Gaunt knew suddenly that there was a way. Whether it would work or not, he didn't know.

These Texans were a peculiar breed. Their code of honor was as rigid as any law ever contrived by man, and not a one of them would break it.

If he could turn the confrontation between him and Wedemeier's entire crew into a confrontation between only Wedemeier and himself. . . . That was the one thing that might work. That would keep the others out of it. That would put him on even terms with one man only, and not only give him a chance to stay alive but also give him a chance of getting the cowboys' guns away from them afterward.

With his course decided, he touched his horse's sides with his heels and rode north across the tracks, turning then and positioning himself between Wedemeier's crew and the town of Cottonwood.

Like a rock he sat there, a tall man on a tall horse, letting it be known that they would have to ride over him before they could get into town.

There was the briefest, slightest hesitation in Wedemeier as he saw him take his position there. Then he came on, a little faster and certainly more confident. He had more than fifteen men. Gaunt was alone. As Wedemeier saw it, there could be but one outcome to the confrontation.

Closer and closer they came, and suddenly all sound among the spectators ceased. The only sounds remaining were the muffled shouts of the men loading cattle into the waiting cars and the protesting bawls of the cattle themselves. In town, a whisper could have been heard on Kansas Street.

Fifty feet away, Wedemeier stopped. He called, "Get out of the way, Marshal, or we'll run over you."

Gaunt knew he couldn't deal with Wedemeier at a distance of fifty feet. He put up a hand and cupped it behind his ear. "Too much noise over there in the cattle pens. What did you say?"

Wedemeier came on. Gaunt wanted him less than a dozen feet away.

There seemed to be no fear in the trail boss. Gaunt realized that he liked the man and knew he couldn't kill him unless it was the only way. This time Wedemeier came to within fifteen feet before he stopped again.

Gaunt said, "Gentlemen, you're going to have to give up your guns before you go into town."

A man behind Wedemeier yelled, "Yeah, and get ourselves killed by a bunch of crooked gamblers!"

"No gambler killed that man last night. I killed him. And only because he had a gun. He put a bullet into me first." He waited just a moment and then added, "If he'd been unarmed, he'd still be alive."

Another man yelled, "Like hell! We go in with guns or we don't go at all!"

Gaunt shrugged. "Then don't go at all. The town council passed the no-gun ordinance. All I do is enforce."

This was petty, this bickering. But there was nothing petty about the stakes. He changed his tone. "Go on in, boys. There's girls and liquor and gambling. Just give me your guns as you pass, and there'll be no trouble."

He held his breath for an instant, waiting to see if they would comply. There was some slight hesitation among them, and several looked back and forth from one to another. In the end it was the words of one hothead that decided them. "No, by God! I ain't giving up my gun!"

That brought a grumble of agreement from the others. Gaunt looked at Wedemeier. "Are you the trail boss or is he?"

Slight color touched Wedemeier's weathered face and his eyes narrowed almost imperceptibly. He said, "You know who trail boss is. You don't have to ask."

"Then why's he giving the orders?"

Wedemeier shook his head. "It won't work, Gaunt. You can't divide us that easily."

Gaunt stared straight at Wedemeier. "All right, then. I'm making it personal. Between you and me. Give me *your* gun, right now, before you go into town."

Wedemeier's face was as nearly expressionless as a man's face can be, so it couldn't have been his expression that gave away his dismay. Maybe it was a change in his eyes, the merest flicker of the lids. But Gaunt saw it and knew that this part of his strategy at least had won. He repeated, "Your gun, Mr. Wedemeier. I'll take it now."

Wedemeier shook his head. "Not that way either, Gaunt. Take all our guns or take none of them."

Gaunt's expression was sardonic and his eyes never left Wedemeier's. "Afraid, Mr. Wedemeier? Afraid without fifteen men to back you up?"

Wedemeier's rage flared like a grass fire. His left hand held his horse utterly motionless, as if it was made of iron. His right was no more than a couple of inches from the grip of his holstered gun.

Now, what Gaunt had known must happen did. The Texan's code would not permit Wedemeier's men to intervene in a private quarrel, no matter what their sympathies. Uneasily, they reined their horses to right and left, getting themselves out of the field of fire.

Gaunt opened his mouth to taunt Wedemeier with the fact that now he was all alone. Instead he relented and said, "It don't have to be this way, Mr. Wedemeier. I can out-draw and out-shoot you, and you know it. I don't want to kill you. All I want is for you to give up your gun."

But it had gone too far and suddenly Gaunt could see it had. Wedemeier had been challenged and his Texas code, as rigid as that of his men, would not permit him to back down. Not and retain his authority over them.

He said, "No, by God! I won't give up my gun. Not unless I'm dead. So get on with it. Draw, damn you! Draw!"

Gaunt shook his head. "I can't do that, Mr. Wedemeier. You're going to have to draw your gun first."

Wedemeier didn't like that; he didn't like the disadvantage it put him at. Not the disadvantage in what now seemed to be an inevitable fight with Gaunt, but a disadvantage so far as his men were concerned.

He said, "No. You want to enforce the gun ban. You draw first."

Gaunt saw no reason to deprive him of his pride. He nodded. "All right. You're sure this is what you want?"

"I'm sure." There was a kind of grayish pallor in Wedemeier's face. It wasn't fear. It was the knowledge that he was going to die. Within minutes. Maybe within seconds.

Gaunt nodded. "All right. Whenever you're ready, Mr. Wedemeier. But I want it understood . . . if you lose, your men will give up their guns. Today and every day as long as they are here."

Wedemeier nodded his head. "That is

agreed." He turned his head briefly to look at one of his men. "Rafferty?"

"Yes, sir. That is agreed."

Now was the deadly moment, the two men facing each other on mounts forcibly held still by iron hands on their reins.

Gaunt well knew his own speed. He knew Wedemeier could never match it. The only way he could leave Wedemeier alive was to draw more swiftly than he ever had before, swiftly enough so that Wedemeier would have time to think, to see how badly he had been beaten, and to decide that only certain death awaited if he persisted in trying to withdraw his gun, center it on Gaunt and fire it.

His thoughts as he stared at his adversary were bleak and grim. Suppose Wedemeier's stubbornness was stronger than his good sense? Suppose his reflexes were too slow to let him stop with his gun already halfway up?

But he had to try one last time. He said, "I can beat you. I draw a salary because I'm an expert with my gun. It's no disgrace to change your mind."

Wedemeier stubbornly shook his head. In that instant, Gaunt knew he would have to kill this man. No matter how much he hated it. No matter how much admiration he had for the wiry trail boss. No matter what a waste it was.

Disgust touched him, disgust with a job that forced him repeatedly into situations like this one. He said, "All right. Now!" the last word like the crack of a whip.

His body now took over from his mind. With the restraints imposed on it removed. His right hand moved like the head of a striking rattlesnake. He felt the smooth, worn, cool grips of his gun, felt it withdraw from its holster, felt it rise, so incredibly swift it was doubtful if the human eye could have followed its movements. He felt his thumb on the hammer and felt the hammer come back with a click.

It was in line, cocked and ready to fire before Wedemeier had his gun halfway out of its holster.

Gaunt's heart stopped for a split second. His eyes were glued to Wedemeier's hand still forcing the gun up and out of its holster.

It cleared and he heard the click as the hammer came back. And yet, with his own death staring him in the face, he still delayed. There was a chance Wedemeier would desist, that he would look at certain death in Gaunt's hand and eyes, and let his gun drop from his hand.

It was a deadly risk, but Gaunt took it. He raised his own glance to meet Wedemeier's. He didn't say anything; he didn't have to. Wedemeier knew he was a dead man unless he halted the inexorable rise of his cocked and ready gun.

In Wedemeier's face, suddenly, unexpectedly, Gaunt saw that he had won. Wedemeier was going to give up. He wasn't going to shoot. Gaunt let his glance drop to Wedemeier's gun, cocked but still not level, still not ready for firing.

Wedemeier's hand sagged as though the weight of the gun was too much for it. Then he released the gun, and it fell with a thud into the dust. It could and should have fired, since the hammer was back, but it did not.

Gaunt carefully lowered the hammer of his own gun, spinning the cylinder as he did so that the hammer lowered on an empty chamber. He shoved it into his holster.

There was nothing overbearing, nothing arrogant in his voice as he spoke. It was almost mild, conciliatory. "Let me have your guns, boys, as you ride past. You'll get them back when you leave town."

Wedemeier dismounted, picked up his

gun, lowered the hammer and shoved it into its holster. He remounted and was the first to hand over his gun. Sullenly for the most part, his drovers followed suit.

Once more Gaunt hung as many as he could on his saddle horn, the rest around his neck. He sat motionless as the cowboys and Wedemeier headed uptown toward the bank where Wedemeier could cash his draft and pay his cowboys off.

Most of the people watching from their various vantage points had by now disappeared. Gaunt saw neither Maggie nor Rose.

He had won another skirmish, but he hadn't won the war. Two more herds had arrived yesterday and their cowboys would be coming to town today.

And behind those two was Buck Robineau, crippled by Gaunt's bullet, still undoubtedly swearing his determination to kill Gaunt by whatever means were necessary.

Gaunt rode toward the jail. Last year there would have been an almost intoxicating exhilaration at the thought of confronting Robineau. Today there was only weariness. Robineau was just another chore.

CHAPTER 14

Gaunt unlocked the jail door and went inside. His leg was paining him this morning and it was difficult not to limp. He wished he had a cane to take some of the weight off it, but he knew using a cane would be giving notice to everyone that he was too crippled up to do his job properly.

He stayed in the jail only long enough to hang the guns he had taken from Wedemeier's men on the coat tree. Unburdened, he went back outside and mounted his horse. It surprised him how much difference the lessened weight had on the amount of pain in his leg.

He rode uptown at a walk. What he really wanted was a drink of whiskey, or maybe two, but he didn't want anybody saying that he was drinking in the morning because he was coming apart. He dismounted in front of the Drovers Hotel, tied his horse and went into the dining room. When Josephina came, he ordered coffee.

Wryly, as he sipped it, he wondered why he had come here instead of going to Maggie's place. Maybe it was because he suspected she was going to get after him again about quitting the marshal's job. Maybe this morning he'd had enough tension and conflict and didn't want more.

He nodded at several other diners, finished his coffee and got up. He went out, mounted his horse and headed up Kansas Street to begin his morning rounds.

He saw Maggie looking out the window as he passed her restaurant. There wasn't much he could do but stop and talk. He dismounted at the rail and looped his horse's reins around it. He went inside.

She turned from the window as he entered. There was hurt in her eyes. "I saw you go into the hotel. Would you rather have coffee there than here?"

"How'd you know I had coffee?" He felt trapped and didn't like the feeling.

"The place has windows you know."

"All right. I had coffee." He started to excuse himself by saying he'd needed something from his room. Then he changed his mind. He wasn't going to start lying to justify the things he did.

"I don't suppose you want any more."

"I could use a cup. I'm not rushed for time."

She headed for the kitchen, and he eased himself onto one of the counter stools. It sure wasn't hard to get in bad with a woman. And lately it seemed to be extraordinarily easy with Maggie Conover.

She brought him a cup of coffee and one for herself and sat down next to him. "Hattie Budge says she saw you walking up the street last night late. She says you were limping pretty badly and that a woman was helping you. A saloon girl she thought."

Gaunt stared at her, the corners of his mouth beginning to turn up with a grin. "Rose Navarro." He didn't elaborate. Maggie was prying, trying to supplement Hattie Budge's gossip, and Gaunt didn't think she had any right to pry. Hell, they weren't married yet.

"Isn't she the one who has an interest in the Alamo?"

"She is."

"What . . . ?" Maggie had the grace to blush painfully. She said, "I'm sorry. I have no right to ask."

"I had a scuffle with a couple of men down by the depot. Several shots were fired. None of them hit me, but I opened up my leg wound and it was bleeding quite a bit. Rose helped me up to Doc's to have him rebandage it."

"How did she . . . ? I mean, have you known her long?"

"She's a very old friend."

Maggie's face flushed for a second time. Her mouth firmed, and he knew there were more questions she wanted to ask. He also knew she wouldn't, at least not now.

But she'd be asking questions around town. About Rose Navarro. About her relationship with Morgan. And she'd probably find out. He'd never made a secret of his visits to Rose. Probably most of the men in Cottonwood knew about them, and some of them had probably told their wives.

Maggie was slipping away from him. And along with her the dreams he'd had of permanence, of a family, of living without a continuous threat against his life. He said, "Maggie, she heard the shots down by the depot. She came out to see if I had been hurt. I hadn't, but my leg was bleeding and she insisted that I go up to Doc's. It was a

174

long walk, and she just went along to help.''

She was mollified, but only slightly. She said, ''I heard talk in the restaurant this morning that two more herds had arrived. And that another was close behind. Mr. Robineau's. The one who swore he'd kill you when he came back this year.''

Gaunt nodded. ''That's right.''

''What are you going to do about him? I heard that his arm is crippled from you shooting him last year and that he won't fight fair. One man said he'd probably use a double-barreled shotgun on you.''

Gaunt said, ''Maggie, a year is a long, long time. A man can't stay mad that long. Robineau's probably forgotten all about saying he was going to kill me this year.''

''A man with a crippled arm doesn't forget that fast.''

He knew what she said was true, but he wasn't going to admit it to her. He finished his coffee. ''I've got to go. I've got my morning rounds to make.''

Her voice was mocking. ''To show the town the presence of the law.''

He studied her closely. ''Something like that.''

''Let somebody else do it. Why does it

have to be you?"

"Because there's nobody else."

"Then let them do without."

He said, "Without law, the crooked gamblers, the petty thieves, the prostitutes, the murderers would take over in Cottonwood. Not a cowboy would be safe as long as he had a dollar in his pocket. Not a woman would be safe on the streets. Not a business would be safe from robbery. Not a citizen would dare go out after dark. It would be a jungle, Maggie, with the predators in full control."

"And only you can prevent that from happening." There was now an even stronger mockery in her voice.

But Gaunt didn't let it anger him. He said simply, "Only me." Because it was the truth. He might not be the only man capable of doing what he was doing, but he was the only one currently available. If he gave the town council enough time, they could no doubt get someone to replace him who was equally good. But he had to give them time. He couldn't just go to them and say he was going to quit. Today. Or tomorrow. Or even next week.

She was angry now. Her face was flushed and her eyes sparkled. She said, "Morgan

Gaunt, I said I would marry you, but I will not marry your job! Either you give it up, or you can give up any idea of marrying me!"

It was finally the ultimatum he had expected and he could see that it had slipped out before she'd had time to adequately consider it. But the stubborn set of her mouth and chin said that she would stand by it now that she had issued it.

He didn't want to quarrel with her. The pain in his leg had made him edgy, and he knew he might say things he would later regret. He got up off the stool. He didn't make matters worse and insult her by putting a coin on the counter to pay for the coffee. He just turned to leave.

In a shriller voice than he had ever heard her use she cried, "I mean it, Morgan! I mean every word I've said."

He clenched his fists, knowing nothing could be gained and much could be lost if he turned and answered her. He went out and pulled the door closed behind him without turning and looking at her again. As he unlooped his horse's reins, his back still to the restaurant, he could hear her weeping.

The sound almost made him turn around

and go back in. He forced himself to mount his horse. If he went back, he'd give in before her tears.

He rode up Kansas Street, scowling to himself. Damn it, the job was hard enough these first few days without having to fight Maggie too.

Deeply troubled and lost in thought, he reached Hooker's hayfield without even remembering getting there. He stopped, dismounted, and leaned on the top wire of the fence with a grass stem in his mouth while his horse reached over the fence for a few clumps of tall grass the mower had missed.

It was dangerous letting himself become preoccupied. Sully and Jackson were still someplace in town and they might try to kill him, perhaps before sundown, or they might hire somebody else to do the job. Wedemeier had been humiliated in front of his crew, and while Gaunt didn't think Wedemeier capable of dry-gulching him, it was possible the man would get drunk enough to challenge him. Or one of Wedemeier's cowboys might get ideas of taking the trail boss's quarrel upon himself.

And then there were the two newly arrived herds. Men would be coming into town from those herds, later on today. It was even possible that Robineau, being less than a day's ride from Cottonwood, would come in to see if Gaunt was still marshal here and perhaps try killing him.

No. He couldn't afford preoccupation. He mounted his horse, rode along the edge of Hooker's hayfield to the bed of Cottonwood Creek.

The air was already hot. Sweat ran down Gaunt's back and soaked the underarms of his shirt. He let his horse pick his careful way along the bank of the creek while he kept his ears tuned to each small sound and watched his horse's ears, knowing they would prick toward anything unusual long before he was able to detect its presence by himself.

Faintly he could hear shouts down in the cattle pens, and the protesting bawling of the cattle as they were prodded and forced up the wooden ramps and into the cattle cars. Wedemeier's herd would make an entire train. It would probably pull out for Kansas City or Chicago before sundown today.

At the lower end of town, he left the bed of Cottonwood Creek and rode along the main alley that ran between the cattle pens.

He stopped once to let some yard workers haze a bunch of cattle across toward the waiting cars. He came out at the depot, climbed his horse onto the platform just as he had a thousand times before. He could hear the telegraph key clacking inside the telegrapher's office. He rode past, stepped his horse down off the wooden platform and rode across the tracks.

Ira Blanton, the undertaker, was waiting in front of the jail. Gaunt dismounted, led his horse over into the shade of the box elder tree at the side of the jail and then returned. "Hello, Ira."

"Hello, Mr. Gaunt." Blanton's expression was worried.

"Something the matter?"

"Well, you might say that. Or something will be. That trail boss, Wedemeier, came over to my place a while ago. Gave me a hundred dollars. Said he wanted a bang-up, rip-snortin' funeral for that cowboy you . . . I mean who got killed last night."

Gaunt shrugged. "His privilege. A hundred dollars ought to buy a pretty nice funeral."

"It will. My best casket. The service. The burial. What bothers me is that he wants a procession down the entire length of Kansas

Street. He's hired the town band to walk behind the hearse in full uniform playing the funeral march.''

Gaunt grinned faintly. This was Wedemeier's revenge, both for his killing of the cowboy and for his humiliating the trail boss by outdrawing him and taking away his gun. It was also a calculated attempt to make trouble for Gaunt by stirring up the cowboys from the other herds. He asked, "What time?''

"Late this afternoon. He wants the procession to get to the cemetery just in time to bury the man before the sun goes down.''

Gaunt's grin faded. Wedemeier's timing would insure that all the cowboys from the two other herds would be on hand to witness the entire show. Because that was what it was going to be—a show.

He said, "All right, Ira. Thanks for telling me.''

Blanton walked away uptown. Gaunt hesitated several moments. His leg hurt. He was hurt inside by Maggie's angry words to him earlier. He wanted a drink, and suddenly he didn't give a damn what anybody thought. He could and would handle his job, and by the time two more days had passed, everybody was going to know he could.

He walked slowly along the boardwalk as far as the Alamo. He went inside and walked to the bar. Jim Boatman was tending bar, a short, rotund man with a head almost totally bald. He reached for a beer mug but Gaunt shook his head, and Boatman grabbed a bottle and a glass. He set them in front of Gaunt.

Gaunt dumped the glass halfway full. He gulped it, then waited for the pleasant warmth to spread through his stomach. He asked, "Rose up yet?"

"I haven't seen her. Want me to go up and see?"

Gaunt shook his head. She'd been up as late as he had, helping him.

Boatman said, "I hear Robineau is just south of town."

"That's what I hear. I rode out to talk to the men with the other two herds, but I didn't see Robineau."

"Think he still intends to try killing you?"

"I doubt it. A lot of things cool off in a year's time."

He heard a door close upstairs and turned his head. Rose was standing on the balcony looking down. When she saw him, she came along the balcony and hurried down the stairs. She had fixed her hair but she still wore a wrapper over her nightgown. Rose didn't need to worry about what any man in Cottonwood might say or do in reaction to her appearance in the Alamo. They knew she was Gaunt's woman. They also knew she owned part of the Alamo.

Her face was filled with concern. "Are you all right this morning?"

He nodded.

"Wedemeier's men are in town. Without their guns. I saw some of them from my window. How did you manage that?"

He shrugged. She studied him, a small smile touching the corners of her mouth. "Just like that."

He nodded. She asked, "What about Robineau? Will he reach town today?"

"Probably."

She touched his arm. "I'd say be careful, but it wouldn't change anything. So I'll just wish you luck." Her words were light enough, but there was nothing light or lacking in concern in her eyes. He poured himself another drink and downed that one too.

He bent and kissed Rose on the mouth.

"It's going to be all right. The first two or three days of every season are the worst. When they're over, then I hardly earn my pay."

She said simply, "I'm here if there's anything you need."

"Thanks." He smiled at her, then turned and left the Alamo.

CHAPTER 15

Rose Navarro watched him go. She was not a woman given to tears, but suddenly she felt a flood of them gathering behind her eyes. So that no one would see, she hurriedly crossed the room, ran up the stairs and along the hall to her room. She went in, taking time to carefully close the door behind. Then the dam burst and her tears came in a flood. She threw herself face down on the bed and buried her head in her pillow, her body shaking violently as she wept.

She had to be crazy, she told herself. He wasn't even hers and never would be. He would marry Maggie Conover, and she knew she'd never see him after that, except casually.

She shouldn't care this much. But she did care, and she couldn't help herself. She was hopelessly in love with him, as hopelessly as any schoolgirl, and she was terrified that he was going to be killed.

If only he loved her, really loved her. If only there wasn't Maggie Conover. But he didn't love her, at least not the way he loved Maggie. He wouldn't marry her. But that was her fault, not his. She had made her choice when she accepted her first job in a saloon. Oh God, if only she had made a different choice.

But if she had, she told herself, she would never have met Morgan Gaunt. She shouldn't be sorry. Even though she could never have more of him than she'd already had, and even though she would lose that very soon, she'd had him for a while.

And nothing lasts forever. Nothing. Not even Morgan, who seemed so indestructible. He wasn't indestructible. He had been shot last night in the leg and the bullet that hit his leg could just as easily have penetrated his heart.

Her weeping finally stopped. She got up off the bed, went to the window and looked down into the street, wiping away her tears with a scrap of perfumed handkerchief and occasionally sniffling like a little girl. Right now she wasn't Rose Navarro, who owned a part of the Alamo and who knew how to take care of herself. She was just a broken-hearted and very vulnerable woman, who did not know which way to turn.

The truth was, she was completely helpless and there was nothing she could do. Nothing but wait, and hope. That Morgan would survive. So that he could marry Maggie Conover as he planned.

She told herself bleakly that she was even willing to let Maggie have him. If only he did not get killed.

When he left the Alamo, Gaunt began the rounds of the remaining ten of the town's eleven saloons. All of these were below Texas Street. The Red Dog was the first. In Sully's absence, Kurt Vossler was tending bar. Gaunt crossed to the bar, ignoring the scowls he got from the two members of Wedemeier's crew who were in the place. Vossler also scowled at him. "Whadda *you* want?"

Gaunt shook his head. "Nothing to drink. I just wanted to tell you that at least two more crews are going to hit town today. I'll get their guns, but they're sure to hear about the cowboy who got killed last night."

"That's your problem, not mine. You

were the one who killed him."

Gaunt said, "Don't get smart with me. He wouldn't have come back to town looking for trouble if Jackson hadn't cheated him. I'm just going to warn you once. Run honest games in all your saloons and see it to that none of your girls empty the pockets of the ones who get too drunk."

"Or what?" Kurt asked insolently.

"Or you'll get what Sully and Jackson got."

"You could've killed them, dragging them to the jail that way."

"Too bad I didn't. If I had, I wouldn't have to worry about them trying to back-shoot me today."

Vossler gloated, "You're worried, then. Good. I hope they do get you. Then, by God, we can run this town the way it should be run."

Gaunt didn't reply to that. He turned to leave. "Remember. Cheat one of the drovers, and I'll come down on you. If they don't get to you first."

"What can they do? Without guns?"

"They can get guns. And they can wreck this town, starting with the places that cheated them."

Kurt Vossler didn't reply to that, but his expression said he figured he and his employees could handle any rag-tag bunch of cowboys intent on wrecking the place. Gaunt shrugged slightly and went on out the door.

He visited each of the remaining nine saloons with similar warnings. A few of the saloonkeepers, like Overman, were offended at the suggestion that they would allow cheating in their establishments. To them, Gaunt said, "You can have cheating in your place without being a part of it. All I want you to do is watch extra close. And if any of the cowboys complain, make a fair investigation of their complaints."

He returned to the jail. His leg wound had begun bleeding again from the walking, but riding wouldn't have been easier, getting on and off almost a dozen times. He brought out his straight-backed chair and propped it against the front wall of the jail. He sat down, tilted back and let himself relax.

It was now past noon. He was hungry but he wanted to rest his leg awhile. The newly arrived cowboys could reach town at any time, along with the two trail bosses.

He closed his eyes, realizing how very

tired he was. He supposed his weariness was partly caused by the fact that he'd gotten very little sleep last night. Mostly, though, it was because of his wound. The constant pain wore him down, and the loss of blood had weakened him.

Gaunt never before had allowed himself doubts about his ability to handle the marshal's job. Today, a sudden, fleeting thought crossed his mind, "What if one of their bullets does bring me down?"

Angrily, he put that disquieting thought out of his mind. He'd been marshal here two years. This was the third. He'd faced down a good many men who were intent on killing him, or said they were, and who were armed and drunk enough to be dangerous and unpredictable. He'd survived so far. Why should doubt begin troubling him now?

He heard footsteps on the boardwalk and opened his eyes. Sam Kohn and Lester Ives were approaching him. He reached into his shirt pocket for his Bull Durham sack and made himself a cigarette. He licked it, twisted the ends and stuck it into his mouth as they stopped in front of him. Ives said, "You don't look very worried."

"Should I be?" He was worried, but he

was glad it didn't show.

"You should. You've ordered Sully and Jackson out of town by sundown, and you ought to know they'll try to kill you rather than leave. After the dragging you gave them last night."

"You don't approve?"

Kohn spoke for the first time. "We neither approve nor disapprove. You're the marshal, and you do what you have to do. But you got out of the shooting last night by pure damn luck. That cowboy's bullet could've gotten you in the chest as easily as in the leg. All we want is for you to stay alive."

Gaunt grinned. "Thanks for your concern, gentlemen."

"Don't be sarcastic. We don't want you killed. We wouldn't want it even if we did not depend on you. We like you. We want you to stay alive."

Gaunt nodded, and this time there was warmth in his voice. "Thanks. I'll stay alive. Last night I put myself between that cowboy and the two he was trying to kill. I won't be that foolish again."

"What are you going to do about Robineau?"

Gaunt had been trying to decide that

himself. Now he answered his own question as well as theirs. "First, I guess I'll find out if he still feels the same way he did last year. If he's intent on killing me, I'm not going to let him roam the streets. I'll throw him in jail, and when he's finished his business I'll put him on the train along with his cattle, tied up if necessary to make sure he don't get off and come back here.

"On the other hand, if he's cooled off since last year and has changed his mind about killing me—well, I guess I'll just let him alone. I feel bad about what I did to him. I didn't have any choice, but I still feel bad."

Ives asked, "Are you having trouble with the gun ban?"

"So far I'm not. I've got the coat tree inside the jail loaded down with guns. That cowboy I shot last night—he came and got his gun and made me think he was leaving town. Then he turned around and came back."

"Maybe men like Sully and Jackson wouldn't be so eager to cheat the drovers if they knew they all had guns."

"Maybe. But the council made the decision and passed an ordinance. It's my job to see that it's enforced. If you're having second thoughts, I'd suggest you have another council meeting and reconsider it.''

Kohn peered sharply at him. "What do *you* think of the ban?''

"I think it's a good idea. These cowboys get pretty drunk. And when they get into a drunken argument they use guns if they have them. Thirteen men were killed in Cottonwood last year, eleven of them cowboys. We're doing them a favor by taking away their guns.''

He waited a moment and when neither man spoke, he added, "Besides, the townspeople are safer when there's not so much gunplay in town. It hasn't happened yet, but sooner or later, some innocent bystander, maybe a woman or child, is going to be killed by accident if we allow guns in town. No, gentlemen, I support your gun ban a hundred per cent. Maybe I didn't at first because I could see how much trouble it was going to be for me, but I sure do now.''

Both Ives and Kohn nodded. They smiled, and shook hands with him and went on up the street, their expressions revealing that they were still not completely convinced that he could enforce the gun ban, handle Robineau and keep the peace without getting himself killed. He had the wry thought that they probably would begin looking for a replacement immediately so that if he did get killed they'd have somebody on tap to take his place.

He still had not lighted his cigarette. Now he did, and leaned back, enjoying it. A green-bodied fly buzzed around his head and he made a pass at it with his hand.

He was feeling better now, rested. He finished his cigarette and flipped it out into the street. He was hungry and it was past time to eat. He got carefully to his feet, favoring his wounded leg, which had stopped bleeding.

He turned and locked the jail door. Then, walking slowly, again wishing he had a cane, he started up Kansas Street.

He had to decide, now, whether to eat at Maggie's place or whether to eat someplace else. He didn't really want to see Maggie, and that surprised him. He knew if he went to her place, the same tension would be between them and the same argument would probably come up.

On the other hand, if he ate someplace else, she would accuse him of avoiding her, and the ensuing argument would probably be more intense. Finally, shrugging fatalistically, he headed for Maggie's place.

He tried to favor his leg but it didn't do much good. He could feel warmth spreading from it and knew it had begun to bleed again. He cursed softly beneath his breath because he knew he needed to keep his leg quiet to allow it to heal and there was no way he was going to be able to keep it quiet, in the forseeable future at least.

He reached Maggie's restaurant and went inside. He took a table by the window because he didn't want to sit on a stool. He stretched his wounded leg out straight under the table and waited.

The place had practically emptied after the noon hour. Remaining were Bart Chapman and another cattle buyer, sitting at the counter smoking and drinking coffee. Gaunt nodded at the two of them. "When do you think those other two trail bosses are going to hit town?"

"Middle of the afternoon. We're going to ride out in a little while and see where they are."

"Let me know when you get back."

"Sure. Glad to." They finished their coffee, left some money on the counter and went outside. Gaunt was now the only customer in the restaurant.

He made up his mind that he wasn't going to discuss anything more controversial than the weather with Maggie this noon. She'd had her say and he'd had his, and one or the other had to give way before they could get a dialogue going between them again.

She was cool and impersonal when she came to his table, but she did not call him Mr. Gaunt, which would have meant she intended to be completely inflexible. "What will you have, Morgan?"

"What's the best?"

"I've got fried chicken. And roast beef."

"Fried chicken. And coffee."

She went away. He had only briefly glanced at her face and then had glanced away again. Her mouth was firmly set, her eyes without warmth. Her attitude plainly had not changed.

Sitting there waiting, he realized that unless he was willing to give in to her demands, they were not going to get married at all. She certainly did not intend to modify or relinquish any of her demands.

The realization that he was losing her, or had already lost her, was extremely depressing.

She brought his food and put it down in front of him then hastily retreated to the kitchen where she stayed, as if fearing *he* would start the same familiar argument. He ate quickly, anxious to get out.

When he finished, she still had not come from the kitchen. He left payment for his dinner on the table, got up and hobbled from the restaurant.

He supposed she was watching him from the doorway leading to the kitchen, but he did not look back.

CHAPTER 16

There was a deep feeling of depression in Gaunt as he limped back toward the jail. The quarrel with Maggie saddened him, and the trouble was he didn't know what he could do about it.

He simply couldn't see his way clear to doing what it would take to smooth things over with her. He couldn't quit. He couldn't betray the trust of the townspeople who had given him the job. Neither could he let Maggie dictate to him in such an important matter. Not and remain the man she wanted and said she loved.

This was what he didn't understand. She said she had fallen in love with him because of what he was. Now she wanted to change him as a condition of marrying him.

He shook his head helplessly, unable to understand, knowing, furthermore, that he would probably never understand. It was the inconsistency of woman, about which he'd heard so much but hadn't encountered until now. He cursed softly.

He reached the jail. He sat down in his straight-backed chair, tilted it back against the wall, and made himself a smoke. He lighted it, trying to ignore the continuous, throbbing pain in his wounded leg. He fished his watch out of his vest pocket and glanced at it. It was almost two o'clock.

He dozed, but snapped awake frequently at sounds nearby. Finally, at four, he got up, walked around to the side of the jail where his horse was standing in the shade idly switching at flies with his tail.

He mounted and rode out of town at a walk, heading south. He crossed the railroad tracks, glancing as he did toward the cattle pens.

Most of Wedemeier's cattle had already been loaded. Only one pen remained, and it was being loaded now. The engine at the head of the long string of cars was getting up steam, belching a cloud of black smoke. By the time he got back, the train would be gone and another would be backing into position to load tomorrow with cattle from the other two herds that had not yet reached town.

And all season it would be like this, until the hundreds of cars now waiting on several sidings east of town were gone; until all the other cars that would be arriving daily were also gone. Then, finally, the town would quiet down and become once more a sleepy prairie town, dozing through the winter months.

And what would he be doing when that time came? Gaunt asked himself. Would he be dead, only another marker in the graveyard outside of town? Would he be married to Maggie and settled into some less-exciting, less-dangerous job? Or would he be neither, and still the marshal of Cottonwood, waiting out the quiet months until the huge cattle herds arrived next year?

In the distance he saw a lift of dust and knew it was the cowboys from one of the newly arrived herds approaching him. He was still less than a quarter mile from town when he stopped. He could hang the guns from one crew on his saddle horn, but he'd play hell trying to carry all the guns from two.

They saw him waiting in the middle of the road and came on, about a dozen as nearly as he could tell without actually counting them. He felt the old tension come to him and the excitement that a confrontation always brought.

This was in no way similar to the confrontation with Wedemeier's crew yesterday. These men both knew of the no-gun ordinance, but they also knew the marshal would meet them prepared to enforce it no matter what enforcing it entailed.

They drew their horses to a halt when they reached him and looked at him expectantly. They were like all the Texas cowboys who came up the trail to Kansas, he thought. All wore Texas boots, scuffed and worn and run-over at the heels. They wore mostly homespun pants out of which as much dust and grime as possible had been carefully brushed. All but a couple had creased, clean shirts on, shirts that had been carried all the way from Texas in a "possible" bag that each man used for his personal things. Their hair, beneath their sweat-stained hats, was slicked down with water and carefully combed. Gaunt was willing to bet every one of them had bathed, in whatever water was available, and had on clean underwear. Some had whiskey on their minds. Most were thinking of women first, whiskey afterward.

He looked at Rosen, the trail boss. "Howdy. Welcome to Cottonwood."

The man inclined his head. A few of the cowboys replied cautiously.

Speaking to the cowboys Gaunt said, "There's a new ordinance in town. No guns. You're supposed to turn 'em in at the jail when you arrive and pick 'em up again on your way out."

The trail boss said, "You already told me about it. I also heard one of Wedemeier's men got killed in town last night."

Gaunt nodded. "He picked up his gun and then went back. Claimed a gambler had cheated him. He was trying to shoot it out with both the gambler and the bartender from the place the gambler worked."

"Who shot him? I heard it was you."

"It was." Gaunt was getting a little angry now. He said, "I tried to calm him down, but he wouldn't calm. Shot me in the leg, and that didn't leave me any choice."

One of the cowboys muttered, "I ain't giving up *my* gun."

The trail boss turned his head. "Oh yes you are. You ain't likely to get shot if you haven't got a gun. It's murder if you do." He looked hard at Gaunt. "I figure you'll see that nothing happens to these boys if they do give up their guns."

Gaunt shrugged. "This is a wide-open town. That's the way you boys want it. I can't swear all the gamblers are honest. I can't say all the whiskey is good. I can't say the saloon women or those in the brothels won't rob you if they get a chance. What I can say is that if anything like that happens, you come to me. Don't try to settle it yourself. I'll see that whatever it is gets made right."

The trail boss studied him. Finally he nodded. "Fair enough. Give him your guns, boys."

He handed Gaunt his gun and rode past. His cowboys followed, each pausing and giving Gaunt his gun. He hung the belts over his saddle horn and when that would hold no more, hung the rest around his neck. He watched them. They rode for maybe a hundred yards. Then one let out a whoop and dug spurs into his horse's sides. The animal pounded away, followed by the others, their riders raking their sides with the spurs and whooping excitedly.

Gaunt plodded back toward town in their wake. It had been much easier than he had expected it would be. The drovers from the other herd would probably surrender their guns with no more protest. And that would just leave Buck Robineau.

And Sully and Jackson, both of whom he had ordered to be out of town by the time the sun went down.

They wouldn't go. And neither Robineau nor any of his men would give up their guns.

He rode across the railroad tracks and when he reached the jail, swung wearily from his horse. He carried the guns in. There was no more room on the coat tree, so he laid them down on the cot, doing it carefully because if one of the cowboys had left a shell under the hammer there was a chance a jar might make the gun go off.

He went back outside and sat down. The sun was now low in the west. He tilted his hat forward over his eyes.

He looked idle and half asleep, but beneath the shade his hat provided for his eyes, they were alert and sharp and roving the street ceaselessly. It was getting along toward sundown and he was a stationary target here for any rifleman. Furthermore, if either Sully or Jackson or both of them did manage to kill him, there would be no one capable of bringing them to justice for the crime. Kurt Vossler and his other employees would control the town.

He heard footsteps and glanced up to see Rose coming along the walk. She stopped in front of him, hands on hips, an exasperated look on her face. "Do you have to sit here in the sun like the bull's-eye of a target? Can't you sit inside?"

He grinned. "I could. And that would give them the idea I'm afraid of them."

"You really aren't afraid of them, are you?"

"Of Sully and Jackson? No. Not of *them.*"

"I'd think you'd be more afraid of men like them than of someone like Robineau."

He grinned again. "All right. Let's go inside." He followed her inside, leaving the door open. The sun cast a slanting pattern of orange light through window and door onto the floor inside the jail. He held a chair for her and then sat down on the corner of the desk, favoring his wounded leg. "What brings you down here?"

"Ben Murphy has offered to follow you around tonight. Two pairs of eyes are better than one."

He knew who had talked Ben Murphy into it. He also knew that Ben must realize how dangerous it would be. Ben was also a quarter owner of the Alamo and usually tended bar there at night.

He shook his head, and saw the disappointed look come into her eyes. "Tell him no, but thanks. It's my problem, and I think I can handle it. If I can't, I'll call on him." He had no intention of calling on Ben or anybody else. Neither did he have any intention of letting himself get killed.

She studied him a moment, her fear for him plainly visible in her eyes. Finally she said, "Walk me up to the Alamo. I'll buy you a drink."

Gaunt grinned affectionately at her. This was her way of getting him out of danger, if only temporarily. He could not help comparing it with Maggie's way, and he felt ashamed when Maggie suffered by the comparison. He nodded, still grinning at her. "All right. Best offer I've had all day."

He followed her out, locking the jail door behind. She took his arm, moved in very close to him, and they went up the boardwalk toward the Alamo. Her closeness to him stirred Gaunt even though he knew its purpose, which was to discourage anyone who might shoot at him. She was willing to put herself into the same danger in her effort to protect him. His smile faded, and he looked down at her with more tenderness than he had ever felt before.

They reached the Alamo and went inside. Rose relaxed instantly. She preceded him to a table by the window where they could see out into the street and sat down. Gaunt sat down facing the door with the window on his right and the inside of the saloon on his left. The sun slid behind the building across the street. Not much longer, he thought. The sun would set in another fifteen minutes, and that was the deadline for Sully and Jackson to leave. If he didn't see them leave, he'd have to go looking for them. That would be safer than letting them come looking for him.

Ben Murphy brought them a bottle and two glasses. Gaunt glanced up at him. "I appreciate your offer, Ben. If I should need you, I'll sure call on you."

Ben nodded. He was a heavy man with a noticeable paunch and a shiny bald head above a broad face and a flattened nose. He returned to the bar, not visibly relieved, and Gaunt knew he'd be a good man if he needed one.

He poured a drink for Rose and one for

himself. She was trying to smile at him, but she kept looking worriedly out the window. On a sudden impulse he said, "Let's have supper at the Cattlemen's Hotel."

She glanced at him in surprise. She watched his face a moment, trying to read his expression without much success. Finally, with a faint smile, she asked, "You and Maggie have a spat?"

"Not really. She's after me to quit, and I can't."

"It won't help matters if she sees me with you."

He shrugged.

She thought a moment, then nodded. "All right. What time?"

"Eight-thirty. All the cowboys that are coming ought to be in town by then. And I'll have finished my early rounds."

He finished his drink and got to his feet. "See you later, Rose."

She nodded, still trying to conceal the worry in her eyes.

Gaunt went out. There was shade now on the walk in front of the Alamo, but in places farther down the street the sun still came over the one-story buildings and cast its orange light upon the walk.

There was a crowd of mounted cowboys

in front of the jail. He reached them and one man said, "We saw the signs . . . about no guns in town." There was a kind of wary hostility in the man. He said, "We'll give 'em up for now. But if there's any trouble . . ." He didn't finish.

Gaunt took their guns, one by one, and they rode on up the street, breaking into a wild, whooping gallop before they reached the corner. Gaunt unlocked the jail and took the guns inside, placing these on the desk. He made a mental note to get somebody down here tomorrow to put in nails or pegs to hang them on. By the time the season was in full swing he could be custodian of a couple of hundred guns every night.

Turning, he relocked the door and headed for the Red Dog Saloon. Kurt Vossler was still tending bar. There were half a dozen cowboys in the place and a poker game going at one of the tables with five players of which only two were cowboys. Gaunt stopped to watch a moment, then went to the bar. "Sully and Jackson here?"

"Here? Why should they be here? You ordered them to be out of town by sundown."

Gaunt had the feeling both Sully and

Jackson *were* here. In the backroom. But it was not quite sundown, and he didn't want to press it yet.

He turned and went outside. He could faintly hear a band playing someplace uptown and remembered that Wedemeier had ordered an elaborate funeral procession for the cowboy he had killed last night.

The procession was visible at the upper end of Kansas Street. They must have formed on Fifth beside Hooker's hayfields. The hearse still had not crossed Fourth.

As the band came closer and its music became louder, men and women began pouring from saloons and shops all along Kansas Street until there was a crowd at the curb as big as any that gathered for the Fourth of July parade.

Blanton's hearse, drawn by four gleaming blacks, came first. There was a black surrey immediately behind, containing Wedemeier and a couple of his cowboys, looking uncomfortable in newly bought black suits with celluloid collars and black ties.

Behind the surrey were Wedemeier's remaining cowboys, mounted, riding in a column of twos. These men had not bought new clothes, but had spruced up what they had.

Behind them, whoever wanted to had fallen in afoot. These included some of the cowboys from the other herds, a few prostitutes and saloon girls and even a few barefooted boys, one of whom was yanked unceremoniously out of the procession by an ear as Gaunt watched.

The band, eleven strong, made an ear-splitting racket as it went past in the narrow street. Gaunt received some hard looks from the cowboys. Then the whole thing was gone, leaving only a pall of dust in the street and the diminishing sound of the band.

The crowd began to disperse. The hearse crossed the railroad tracks followed by the surrey and the band, now playing the "Funeral March." The rest of the procession followed, turned left and disappeared.

Gaunt headed for the jail to get his horse. It was time for his evening rounds.

CHAPTER 17

It was a little after sundown when Gaunt mounted his horse to begin his evening rounds. A few high clouds in the west flamed orange, then red, and finally took on shades of lavender before everything turned gray.

He rode up Kansas Street to Goliad, determined tonight to vary the routine of his rounds and so try to throw Sully's and Jackson's timing off. He was certain now in his own mind that they had no intention of leaving town.

He turned right on Goliad before he reached the Red Dog Saloon, peering into the Pink Lady on the corner as he passed. Lamps had been lighted inside, but with the dusk light outside, it was difficult to see anything. He went on, glanced into the Longhorn and then went on to Oak.

Once the sun had disappeared and the clouds had lost their afterglow, darkness settled rapidly over the town of Cottonwood. He rode for a block along Oak, then turned back toward Kansas on Texas Street.

At the alley between Kansas and Oak, Gaunt turned south. The Red Dog was halfway down the block. It was possible he could surprise Sully and Jackson leaving by the rear door and thus get the upper hand. But everything was dark. His horse showed no interest in the area near the back door of the Red Dog. Either Sully and Jackson had already left, or they were waiting until it was even darker than it was now.

He considered waiting a while to see if they would appear but gave the idea up, thinking of the supper he had arranged with Rose and not wanting to keep her waiting.

He returned to Texas Street, rode over to Kansas and beyond, checking the small hotels and shops that lined Texas on the west side of Kansas Street.

He could hear occasional yells from the forty or fifty cowboys who were in town. He could sometimes faintly hear a woman's laughter or the tinkle of a piano. He returned to Kansas and rode up the exact center of the street like a man without a care or an enemy in the world.

Passing the Alamo, he saw Rose standing in the shadows watching him. He pulled aside and halted. She asked, "Do you have to ride in the middle of the street?"

"Always have. It makes things easier for me to see."

She knew what he meant by "things." Drunks with guns who thought they had reason to try killing him. Or sober men, who really did have reason and who, because they were sober, were deadlier.

He said, "Eight-thirty," and she nodded her head at him, her face in shadow so that he could not see what expression it wore. He went on, past the Cottonwood Bank to Maggie Conover's restaurant which was always very busy at this time of night.

He felt guilty when he saw Maggie standing in the doorway watching for him. She would be expecting him for supper when his rounds were finished, and he wouldn't be coming tonight. Moreover, it was possible, even likely, that she would find out he was having supper with Rose instead.

He caught himself regretting the invitation he had issued to Rose on the spur of the moment, and then he felt guilty because of his regret. He made a rueful grimace thinking, "Damn it, you're still a free man. You can do as you please."

He halted his horse. Maggie was hot from the kitchen and there was the shine of perspiration on her smooth forehead. He said, "Evening, Maggie."

Her words rushed out, "I'm sorry, Morgan. I wanted to tell you that. That's why I was waiting here for you."

"It's all right, Maggie. It's all right." But he wasn't sure it was.

She said, so softly he could scarcely hear, "I know tonight will be dangerous for you. I will pray for you."

"Thank you, Maggie." Her words had made him ashamed of the thoughts that had been running through his head. Almost hurriedly, he turned his horse and went on up Kansas Street without looking back.

A dog ran out to bark at him. He spoke to it and the animal stood there watching him, idly wagging his tail. Gaunt felt himself relax. No one would hide in the bushes along Kansas Street. Because of the dogs. Anyone skulking there would be discovered and barked at by the dogs.

His mind went on. Hooker's hayfield? He doubted it. There was little cover at the upper end of town and none north of Hooker's fence because of the fact that the hay had been mowed so recently.

He reached Hooker's fence and turned toward the bed of Cottonwood Creek. He could have turned the other way, but he didn't really want to avoid the ambush he knew Sully and Jackson might have set for him because avoiding it would only postpone the attempt until later on tonight.

Not the bed of Cottonwood Creek, then. It was too completely dark down there. They'd have to shoot at the sounds his horse made moving through the brush and that would not be certain enough to satisfy either one of them.

Where, then, for God's sake? And suddenly he knew. The same place they'd used last night. Neither of them were devious or particularly smart, but it *would* occur to them that the place he'd least expect them to use would be the same place they'd used last night.

Riding along the bed of Cottonwood Creek, he could feel the old, familiar excitement rising in him at the prospect of an encounter with Sully and Jackson in which the stakes would be life itself.

Sourly he thought that it was this kind of

excitement in men that made war possible, even inevitable. It was what insured continuous conflict among individual men. Well, whether he liked it or not, he knew now that he couldn't live on this kind of excitement all his life, no matter who he married or did not marry. He would have to find some other way of making a living because this way only had one end. Death.

The phrase that had run through his thoughts, "No matter who he married," came back to him, and he admitted for the first time that he was beginning to have profound doubts about marrying Maggie Conover at all. And for the first time he openly admitted to himself that marriage to Maggie wasn't going to work, no matter how much he loved her, no matter how much she said she loved him.

He felt almost as though she had suddenly been taken away from him. He felt saddened and depressed. He cursed softly to himself and made his mind return to Sully and Jackson, waiting up ahead of him, waiting to shoot him down.

Maggie was right about one thing. It *was* time he quit. It had gotten so he couldn't keep his mind on the job any longer, not to the extent that was necessary to insure survival.

He reached the place in Cottonwood Creek where he always climbed his horse out of it. It was pitch black now, with the only light that small amount coming from the stars. The horse lunged up the steep path made by his own hoofs over the past couple of years. Ahead, Gaunt could see the cattle pens dimly in the darkness. The last train had left, carrying with it the last of Nick Wedemeier's herd. Wedemeier and his men would all be going back to Texas soon, probably in the next two or three days. It didn't take long for the saloonkeepers, gamblers and prostitutes of Cottonwood to relieve the drovers of the wages they'd received for the long drive north. The cowboys would ride south, broke, living off the country as they went, until they reached whatever place they had started from this spring.

He stopped briefly at the edge of the cattle pens, listening. The cowboy mourners had long since returned from the cemetery and were now drowning whatever sorrow they felt over the loss of a comrade in the cheap liquor served in the town's saloons. The hearse had been put away, the band had taken their pay and dispersed.

The faint sounds of revelry from the town's saloons reached him on a light northwest breeze. He touched his horse's sides with his heels and rode on, tense now and ready, as dangerous as a teased rattlesnake. His right hand was never more than two inches from the grips of his holstered gun. His left was high, holding the reins, feeling through them every slight movement of his horse's head. The horse's ears, invisible in this complete darkness, weren't the only things that would warn him of an alien presence. The horse's head would do the same, if Gaunt himself was alert enough.

He rode along the alleyway that separated the scores of individual pens. The smell of manure was fresh and steamy tonight from the cattle that had been shipped out of here today. A new line of boxcars stood opposite the loading chutes, waiting for tomorrow's herd or herds.

Robineau. Gaunt hoped that time had cooled Robineau's hatred, but he doubted it. At least Sully and Jackson would be out of the way by the time Robineau hit town. Unless he came in tonight. Unless he couldn't wait.

Angrily he put that thought out of his

mind. He could see the railroad depot ahead now, with the ever-present square of light visible where Jim Sutton's window was. That was where the danger was; that was where they'd hit him. But in spite of that certainty, his alertness did not relax as he approached the end of the alley between the pens.

The gate at the end of the alleyway was closed and he cursed softly to himself. It squeaked when opened or closed and the squeak would warn the two waiting at the depot for him. But there wasn't any help for it because there wasn't any other way of getting out of the cattle pens other than going all the way around, and he was too stubborn to do that.

Without dismounting, he drew back the bar that secured the gate and swung it wide. He turned his horse, closed the gate and secured it again with the bar. As he had expected, the gate squeaked thunderously.

He was now more tense than he could remember being before. One killer after his hide was bad enough. Two was worse.

He reached the depot platform. Now, he told himself, was the time to deviate routine. He damned the pride that wouldn't permit it. He stepped his horse up onto the platform and headed for the square of light that came from the telegrapher's window. He was thinking that he wouldn't give them the satisfaction of making him vary his routine, and then, as quickly as he had that thought he had another, which was that he was being a goddamn fool. Unnecessarily. When your life is at stake, when you are dealing with killers who will shoot you from ambush, there is no shame in trying to protect yourself and stay alive. With death so near, he had a fleeting thought of someone else, and oddly enough, it was of Rose he thought and not of Maggie. He had a supper date with Rose, and no damned foolishness on his part was going to make him fail to keep it.

He was now ten feet from the window, and suddenly his horse's head turned slightly to the right and his ears pricked forward. They were there, all right, just where they had been last night, just where he had expected them to be tonight.

He was less than five feet from the window's near side, almost too late to do anything to protect himself. Almost. He left his horse at the same instant a volley of shots racketed from the darkness on his right less than twenty feet away.

He thought for an instant that he had caught his right boot heel on something as he swung from the saddle, but almost instantly he realized it had not caught at all but had been ripped away by a bullet fired from one of his assailants' guns. His wounded leg hit the station platform and collapsed, just as another two shots racketed, the bullets tearing splinters from the depot walls.

Gaunt's horse let out a snort of surprise and pain, gathered his haunches under him and sprang forward, across the shaft of light streaming from the telegrapher's window to disappear into the darkness beyond. His passage drew yet a third volley from the darkness, and the gun flashes from this volley registered in Gaunt's mind as he drew his own gun and thumbed the hammer back.

His horse was hurt; he knew that for a certainty. The animal was too steady to spook at simple gunfire unless he had been hurt by it.

The knowledge further angered him. So did the freshly throbbing pain in his wounded leg, which had given way under him. He fired, aiming his first shot a little higher than the gun flash that still seemed

222

seared onto his eyeballs and a little to his right.

It is sometimes possible to hear a rifle bullet hit either a man or an animal, but this range was too short. The revolver's report obscured the sound the bullet made striking flesh.

Yet somehow Gaunt knew his bullet had struck its mark, and he turned his gun on the second ambusher, who obliged him by firing at him again. But so nervous was this ambusher that, instead of hitting Gaunt, he hit the telegrapher's window and the shards of broken glass showered down onto the station platform.

Jim Sutton was probably already flat on the floor, thought Gaunt even as his gun centered on this unexpected new target, pulled right a little and bucked against his palm. This shot was followed, so closely a man might think he had imagined it, by an explosive grunt, as though the bullet's impact had driven a gust of air from the man it struck.

Suddenly all was silent. There was no sound from where all the bullets had been fired. There was no sound from inside the telegrapher's office. The shards of glass had by now all fallen, and Gaunt's horse had crossed the tracks, probably not stopping until he reached the jail.

Gaunt could hear his own breath sighing in and out. He was pretty sure both Sully and Jackson were out of action, but he didn't intend to take any unnecessary chances finding out.

He waited for what seemed an eternity. Then he heard Jim Sutton's shaky voice, "Mr. Gaunt? Are you all right?"

"I'm all right, Jim. You got a lantern in there?"

"Sure, Mr. Gaunt. Want me to bring it out?" He sounded scared and reluctant.

"Yeah. It'll be all right. I'll cover you."

His voice had drawn no shots, further reinforcing his belief that the two were dead. He punched out the empties in his gun by the faint glow of light from the window, then replaced them with fresh cartridges. Sutton appeared at the doorway leading onto the platform from his office, a lighted lantern in one hand.

Gaunt didn't look at him. He was looking out beyond the station, toward the place from which the shots had come. He could now make out two prone bodies, neither of which moved.

Sutton stepped down off the platform,

holding the lantern high and squinting, trying to see. Gaunt headed for the two bodies on the ground.

The first thing he did was get their guns. Then he knelt to make sure neither was alive.

Jackson was dead. Sully was breathing, but weakly and raggedly. Gaunt got painfully to his feet. "One of them is dead. The other one likely will be soon, but I suppose I'd better get Doc to look at him."

"Want me to go after Doc?"

"I'd appreciate it. I've got to see how bad my horse is hit."

Sutton hurried away up the street. Gaunt hobbled painfully toward the jail, hampered now not only by his wounded leg but by a missing bootheel on the other foot.

CHAPTER 18

The gunfire down at the depot had brought a crowd out of the saloons at the lower end of town. Cowboys from the three herds that had already arrived began to fill Kansas Street, a few girls, bartenders and gamblers scattered among them. Sutton reached them first and answered their excited questions. He went on through, heading for the doctor's house. Gaunt plodded across the tracks and up the lower end of Kansas Street to the jail. No questions were asked of him as he passed through the dispersing crowd, for which he was grateful. He reached the jail.

His horse stood trembling at the hitching post in front. Gaunt went inside and lighted a lantern. He carried it outside. He held it high while he went over his horse for wounds.

Blood had congealed on the horse's hip. He found a gouge in the horse's rump about two inches long and a quarter of an inch deep. It wasn't a clean wound such as would have been made by a bullet, but ragged and torn. It must have been made by his bootheel, Gaunt thought, after it had been torn off by the bullet. The horse would have a scar, but the wound wasn't serious, not serious enough to require the attention of Lucas Thorne, the veterinarian. He could handle it himself.

Gaunt mounted and rode the still trembling animal up the street to the Drovers Hotel. He tied his horse to the hitching post, went inside and climbed the stairs to his room without glancing at the clerk or at any of the other occupants of the lobby. It was hard to walk with one leg throbbing so painfully and the bootheel gone from the other foot. He was relieved to reach his room.

He got another pair of boots out of the closet. Using the bootjack, he pulled off both boots, then sat down on the edge of the bed and put the others on.

Robineau would be in town by now, he thought—or would be soon. And despite what he had told Rose about Robineau forgetting his grudge, he didn't expect it to happen. When he went out, he'd have Robineau to face, if not right away, then later tonight.

There was a wet spot on Gaunt's trouser leg where blood had seeped through the bandage, but he didn't feel up to changing his pants just now. He blew out the lamp, settled his hat on his head, and went out into the hall.

He was better able to walk now, and managed to make it down the stairs and across the lobby to the outside door without limping too noticeably. Everybody in town knew he had been shot, of course, and expected him to limp. He just didn't want to limp so badly that anyone would get the idea he couldn't do his job.

On the hotel veranda, he encountered Ives and Kohn, both wearing worried expressions. Ives said, "Robineau is here. In town."

Gaunt nodded.

"With about half his crew," said Kohn.

"And they've all got their guns, I suppose."

Both men nodded. "Yes. We think you ought to raise a posse. It's the only way you're going to be able to get their guns away from them."

Gaunt shook his head. "Not the only way."

Kohn looked at him exasperatedly. "You don't have to face every troublemaker one-to-one. He wants to kill you, man!"

"So did Jackson and Sully. So have a lot of others."

"But . . ."

"Gentlemen, I appreciate your concern. And I think I will quit at the end of the year."

"We'll need a police force to take your place!"

Gaunt grinned. "If you'll excuse me, gentlemen, I haven't eaten yet." He went down the veranda steps and headed across the street toward the Alamo.

Rose Navarro, with her ears sharply tuned for the sounds of pistol shots, heard the volleys that sounded like strings of fire-crackers down by the depot at the lower end of Kansas Street.

An icy hand seemed to clutch her heart. She waited, heard several more shots, then hurried through the crowd to the door and stepped outside.

She looked down the street in the direction

from which the shots had come. She couldn't see anything but a scattered crowd of men and women who had come curiously from the saloons to see what was going on.

She realized that her knees were trembling. She forced herself to go back inside because she knew there was nothing she could do out here. She couldn't help Morgan Gaunt no matter how much she wanted to. She could only wait. And if he survived, she could watch him marry Maggie Conover and turn forever away from her.

Bitterness touched her briefly and then went away. She couldn't blame Morgan for the way things were and she couldn't blame Maggie Conover. They only one she could blame was herself.

But she didn't have to go on this way. She didn't have to stay in the saloon business until she was old and wrinkled and hard. She could get out now and maybe, in time, she could attain some kind of respectability. Even if she could not have Morgan Gaunt.

Ace Kenyon, who owned the other half of the Alamo, was behind the bar tonight. She called to him, "Ace. I want to talk to you."

As she led the way to a corner table, she glanced at the big clock behind the bar. It was a little after eight. She was supposed to have supper with Morgan at the Cattlemen's at eight-thirty, and she didn't even know if he was still alive.

Ace held a chair for her and then pulled one out himself. He straddled it, his arms resting on its back. Rose knew Ace liked her and would probably marry her if it wasn't for Morgan Gaunt. And she liked Ace. But not that way.

He asked, "What's on your mind?"

"I want to sell my share in the Alamo."

"Why? It's a good living."

"I want to sell. Do you want it or shall I look for somebody else?"

"I want it. You paid fifteen hundred. I'll give you two thousand."

Rose nodded. "Have the papers drawn up."

He studied her puzzledly. "Mind telling me why? Is it Morgan Gaunt?"

She nodded dumbly, unable to trust herself to speak. She could feel the tears building up like a flood behind her eyes.

"I thought he was going to marry Maggie Conover."

That was exactly what she hadn't needed

to hear right now. She got to her feet, tears now spilling out of her eyes. She opened her mouth to tell him that she didn't give a damn what he thought, then closed it without saying anything. She turned and hurried toward the stairs, colliding with several patrons between the table and the foot of the stairs. She went up, ran along the hall to her room, went in, slammed and locked the door.

She was a fool. Morgan might already be dead. Even if he was not, he was not for her. Nor was respectability. Nobody would ever let her forget what she was or what she had been. With tears running silently down her cheeks she went to the window, opened it and stuck her head out so that she could see down toward the lower end of the street.

She felt weak with relief when she saw Morgan on his big chestnut horse. He sat straight, and seemed to be all right.

Trembling violently, she withdrew from the window and sat down in her chair before her mirror. He would be coming to take her to supper soon. And she wanted to look her best.

Before Morgan Gaunt got to the jail, he met Blanton's hearse going up the street.

He stopped, and Blanton stopped. Blanton said, "I thought there was supposed to be two."

Gaunt shook his head. "Only one. The other was still alive."

"Well, Doc didn't find him. He must've crawled away someplace."

Gaunt knew he didn't have much time. But if possible he wanted to know where Sully was and how badly he was hurt. Most of all he wanted to know how much of a threat Sully was.

He rode as far as the jail where he stopped and picked up the lantern. He didn't light it, but mounted and rode to the place where the shooting had taken place. He scouted around in the darkness to make sure Sully wasn't close enough to kill him the minute he struck a match. Then he lighted the lantern, went to where the two had fallen, and by lantern light studied the ground.

The wheel tracks of Blanton's hearse were clearly visible as were the boot tracks of those who had helped load Jackson's body into it. Gaunt paid no attention to these. He was looking for the marks Sully must have made dragging himself away from the scene, and he found them and followed them. They went as far as the loading pen fence. Here, Sully had apparently pulled himself to his feet. His boot tracks led away from here. He had been staggering, but he obviously was a long ways from being dead.

Gaunt went back to his horse, more disturbed than he would have liked to admit. Now he not only had Robineau and half that man's crew, but he had a wounded and possibly dying Sully, who, if he did not collapse and die between here and town, would also be gunning for him. Sully, if he had as much strength as he appeared to have, would be as dangerous as a wounded grizzly bear, filled with hate and pain, wanting only to satisfy it by killing the man who had hurt him so.

Gaunt blew out the lantern and mounted his horse. The animal seemed to have calmed considerably and was no longer trembling. Gaunt rode back to the Drovers Hotel, where he washed his face and shaved. Now, he took the time and effort to change his pants and shirt and comb his hair. Then he went back down the stairs.

He left his horse tied at the hitch rail in front of the Drovers and walked across the street. The noise from the saloons had picked up as the cowboys began getting drunk. Half a dozen tinny pianos now filled the street with their music, discordant because not one single tune could be separated from the rest.

Gaunt crossed the street to the Alamo. Ace Kenyon was behind the bar. Gaunt crossed to it and Ace slid him a bottle and a glass. Gaunt poured himself a drink. As he downed it, Ace said, "I'll send for Rose. She's up in her room."

"Thanks." Gaunt wanted another drink but he denied himself. He needed quick reflexes in the night to come.

Ace said, "You're a lucky man."

Gaunt didn't know whether he was referring to Maggie or to Rose. So he didn't say anything.

Ace said, "I'd marry Rose myself if she'd have me."

Still Gaunt didn't say anything. He just looked at Ace, who quickly said, "Ain't none of my business, of course. But she's a fine woman, although I expect you know that without me telling you."

"I do." Something made him turn his head and he saw Rose coming down the stairs.

She was beautiful, dressed in a long, pale lavender gown with a low neckline that showed the creaminess of her throat and upper breasts. He crossed the room to her and she took his arm, trying to smile, trying to blink back the tears that brightened her eyes. She said tremulously, "I thought . . . I heard those shots and . . ."

He said, "It's all right. It's all right."

"Yes." Her smile was brighter now as he walked her out the door into the street. She clung tightly to his arm, keeping her body very close to him as if she knew there was less chance of anyone shooting at him with her so near.

From habit, Gaunt scanned both sides of the street as they walked north toward the Cattlemen's. His glance searched each darkened passageway, each doorway deep enough to hide a man. No drovers were supposed to be above Texas Street, but that didn't mean none of them could be here. Besides, the deadline didn't apply to Sully, who could go anyplace in town he pleased.

The Cattlemen's Hotel was directly across Kansas Street from Maggie Conover's restaurant. Examining his own inner conscience, Gaunt wondered whether he had not had an ulterior motive in asking Rose to supper with him tonight and had picked the Cattlemen's deliberately so that Maggie would see him on the street with Rose.

If he had, he admitted to himself, it was nothing of which he could be proud. If he intended to break with Maggie, he should do it cleanly and face-to-face, not by letting her see him with Rose instead.

But he really hadn't been that devious. The invitation to Rose had been issued spontaneously, with no thought of any possible consequences.

He didn't look in through the windows of Maggie's restaurant as they passed. Neither did Rose. They went on, reached the corner, crossed the street and climbed the steps to the veranda of the Cattlemen's Hotel. Robineau would probably be staying here, he thought, since it was the best in town and also since the Texas Street deadline did not apply to trail bosses as it did to their men. Trail bosses had to come north of Texas Street to transact their business.

They entered the lobby, in which there were few people tonight. Gaunt was conscious of the stares they drew. Everybody in town knew he was courting Maggie. Everybody also knew he was seeing Rose.

She was watching him, her eyes very steady and calm. She said, "You could have crossed the street. Then Maggie probably wouldn't have seen."

He didn't know what to say to that. But Rose wouldn't let it go. "When are you going to marry her?"

Suddenly, confronted with that question, he finally and squarely faced the truth. "I'm not."

Surprise showed in her face. "But why? I thought . . ."

He said, "It wouldn't work. I thought it would, but I was wrong."

She kept her glance downcast now. Gaunt was already thinking ahead. After supper he'd deposit Rose immediately at the Alamo where she would be safe. He wouldn't subject her to any further dangers by being seen with her on the street. Not until both Sully and Robineau were accounted for.

Rose was afraid to look up at him. Her heart had begun to beat with an almost painful rapidity when he'd said he wasn't going to marry Maggie after all. She was sure he could feel her hand trembling upon his arm.

In her eyes was the old fear for his safety that was always there. But now there was something else, a wild kind of joy. At least, if he survived the night, she was not going to lose him. Anyway not yet.

CHAPTER 19

The Cattlemen's Hotel had been copied after the Stockyards Hotel in Chicago. Its lobby was a hundred feet long and nearly fifty feet wide. It was liberally sprinkled with brown leather-covered sofas and chairs, and against the wall there were many writing desks and chairs. There must have been at least a hundred polished brass spittoons in the lobby, which was floored with white tile and covered with a scattering of large and beautiful Indian rugs. The walls were hung with the stuffed heads of moose, elk, bear, deer and mountain lions along with pictures of Buffalo Bill Cody, Sitting Bull, John Brown, Lincoln and various other well-known figures of the time, alive and dead.

The dining room was even more elegant than the lobby if that was possible. Linen tablecloths covered every table. The walls were of paneled oak and the carpet underfoot was a rich wine color. A candle burned on each table, but the crystal chandeliers, of which there were two, provided most of the light.

They were ushered to their table by a man in a starched white jacket, who held Rose's chair for her while she sat down. Gaunt stretched out his wounded leg as he sat down, then looked at Rose over the candle burning on the table.

She was very lovely by candlelight but then, he thought, she was very lovely in any light. Her life, whatever it had been, had touched her little, and suddenly he knew what he was going to do. But not yet. Not until he had decently broken off with Maggie.

He ordered absently after consulting Rose about what she wanted to eat. The white-coated Negro waiter brought red wine in a napkin-wrapped bottle and poured it carefully. Rose raised her glass, her face showing no humor and no cynicism but only sober concern. "To tomorrow."

He touched his glass to hers, smiling. "Don't worry so. I told you it was going to be all right."

She sipped her wine, then put the glass down. For an instant she said nothing and it was as though she was gathering her thoughts. Finally she said, "How can you be so sure? Do you know something the rest of us don't?"

"No," he replied soberly. "I just have confidence in myself."

"You were hit in the leg last night, and that wound may kill you yet if you don't take care of it."

"I did something I knew was foolish last night. I won't do that again."

"Why did you do it last night?"

"I miscalculated. I thought the cowboy wouldn't shoot. He didn't have anything against me."

"He was drunk. And drunks don't behave like sober men."

He said, "I'll be careful of drunks tonight."

She stared at him with exasperation. "I don't want to badger you. You get enough of that . . ." She stopped, embarrassed by what she had been about to say. She finished lamely, "Just be careful. Just think before you put yourself into danger."

"All right." He reached across the table and covered her hand with his own. Her glance raised and her eyes met his, holding them almost desperately for a long, long time. Then she looked away and Gaunt removed his hand.

The waiter brought their dinner. Gaunt was preoccupied as he ate, not the cheerful companion he had wanted to be to Rose. She watched him whenever she could without getting caught at it. Her eyes sometimes were bright with tears, sometimes dry and angry, but always they held her deep concern for his safety throughout this crucial night.

The supper was finally finished. Gaunt paid the bill and rose. Rose took his arm leaving the dining room. Crossing the street she said, "Ace is buying my interest in the Alamo."

He glanced down at her with surprise, his eyes questioning.

Almost defensively she said, "I'm tired of it."

He opened his mouth to ask her what she would do, then closed it without saying anything. He was no fool and he wasn't blind. He knew what Rose wanted to do. But he wouldn't ask her now, tonight, when there was a chance he wouldn't live to see the dawn. He had minimized the danger to him from Robineau, Robineau's crew and the wounded Sully to Rose, but he couldn't minimize it to himself.

He took her inside the Alamo. She asked, "A drink?"

He shook his head. "I'll see you later on tonight."

Unexpectedly she stood on tiptoe and, pulling his head down, kissed him on the mouth. She said something she had never said before, "God go with you and keep you safe."

Gaunt turned and limped out of the Alamo. Rose watched him go, as if sure she would never see him again.

Gaunt stood for a moment on the walk in front of the Alamo. He glanced uptown and saw Maggie leaving her restaurant. She turned and locked the door. She glanced down the street, saw him, then deliberately turned her back and headed up the street toward home.

She had seen him with Rose, he thought, probably when they went to supper and also when they returned. He supposed he ought to catch up and walk her home, but he didn't move. He had enough on his mind tonight without doing what he knew had to be done eventually, breaking off with Maggie. She had, in fact, virtually broken off with him already by issuing the ultimatum that he either quit the marshal's job or they were through.

Standing there, he forced himself to put both Maggie and Rose completely out of his mind. Tonight he needed complete concentration if he expected to see the dawn.

His horse was standing at the hitch rail in front of the Drovers Hotel where he had left him earlier. He crossed the dusty street, avoiding a freight wagon, untied and mounted his horse. This was easier on his leg since he could avoid putting any weight on it except when the horse was trotting. At a walk, his wounded leg could be completely relaxed.

All right. First things first. That meant making the rounds of the saloons and relieving Robineau's men, one by one, of their guns. There was a chance Robineau would be in any saloon he entered, and so he would have to proceed more carefully than he ever had before.

He was counting on the loyalty of Robineau's men to make his relieving them of their guns possible. They knew Robineau wanted the marshal for himself. The crippled trail boss wasn't going to take it kindly if one of his men eliminated the marshal before Robineau had a chance at him.

Kurt Vossler's saloons would be the most dangerous, he thought. So he'd hit them first. Starting with the Red Dog, where Vossler was tending bar. After that, he'd take them one by one as he came to them.

He had a sudden idea and grinned at it. With no little anticipation, now, he headed down Kansas Street toward the Red Dog, just below Texas Street.

There were a few cowboys on the board-walks. Several girls lounged in the doorways of the cribs across the street, sometimes calling out invitingly to one of the passing cowboys.

Gaunt turned his horse. He rode up on the boardwalk and, bending low as he did, rode his horse straight into the smoky, noisy saloon.

The noise stopped instantly. Kurt Vossler stared for an instant in amazement. Then his face got red and he roared, "What the hell do you think you're doing?"

Gaunt said, "Some of these cowboys still have guns. I want them. Now."

His horse, used to jumping up onto the station platform every night showed no particular nervousness at the hollow-sounding wooden floor underneath his hoofs. But the smoky air and the crowd made him nervous. Gaunt repeated, "Your guns, gentlemen. I want your guns. You all saw the notices posted outside of town. You should have stopped and left them at the jail."

A red-haired, stocky cowboy said, "Wasn't nobody there."

Gaunt glanced at him. "You one of Robineau's?"

The red-haired man grinned. "Sure am. I'll bet you'd like to know where he is right now."

"I'll find him."

"You sure as hell will!"

Gaunt said patiently, "Give me your guns. You can pick them up at the jail when you leave town."

He watched Robineau's three men, the ones with guns, carefully as they unbuckled their gun belts. He said, "Rebuckle the belts so I can carry them over my saddle horn."

The red-haired one said, "To hell with you. Do it yourself."

Gaunt looked the man squarely in the eyes. He let his stare hold that of the cowboy for almost a full minute. When he spoke, his voice was curt. "Buckle them."

The cowboy looked at his companions, right and left. For an instant, Gaunt could see he was considering drawing the gun and making a fight of it.

His own hand moved very slightly. When it stopped it was less than half an inch from the grips of his own holstered gun. He repeated, "Buckle them." He could have done it himself, of course. But he couldn't let the cowboy get the upper hand.

From behind the bar, Vossler grumbled something and moved, as if to reach under the bar. Instantly Gaunt's gun was in his hand. The hammer made a click as it came back. His voice was like a whip. "Put your hands on the bar."

Vossler did, his forehead shining suddenly with sweat. It was the end of the cowboys' resistance, too. With Gaunt's gun covering them, they now had no choice but to comply. They buckled the three belts and each man handed his belted gun up to Gaunt.

Gaunt hung them on the saddle horn. He backed his horse out of the saloon. The animal jumped nervously when his rump touched the swinging doors but he backed on out, and Gaunt ducked to avoid hitting his head.

He heard the grumbling comments as he turned away toward the next saloon. "Dirty, uppity son-of-a-bitch!" and, "Wait'll he meets up with Buck."

He smiled faintly and without humor as he moved on down the street. He did not minimize the danger he faced tonight. It was greater than any he had ever faced before.

But it would, if he survived it, have its rewards. With Sully and Robineau in jail, keeping order in Cottonwood ought to be easy for the rest of the season. Particularly if he got an opportunity to meet both Robineau and Sully face to face.

A man passed him, hurrying, the red-haired cowboy who had given him an argument back in the Red Dog Saloon. He watched where the man went, able to follow his progress along the darkened street by the light coming from the windows and open doors of the various saloons. The man turned the corner on Goliad, almost running.

Gaunt kicked his horse in the sides and the startled animal leaped ahead, galloping instantly. Gaunt pounded around the corner of Goliad and Kansas, the hoofs of his horse thundering on the hard-packed ground. Dust rose behind him in a cloud.

He saw the red-haired cowboy disappearing into another of Kurt Vossler's saloons, this time the Gold Coin. He saw a man who looked like Moss, the gambler from the Pink Lady running along the street. This man also disappeared into the Gold Coin Saloon.

Gaunt wondered where Sully was. In the Gold Coin too, he supposed. Were they waiting for him there, all of them? Robineau? Sully? Moss? And as many of Robineau's cowboys he had been able to talk into helping him. Three men at least. Six or eight at the most. And one, Robineau, would be armed with a scatter-gun.

Riding into the Gold Coin would be suicide. Walking in would be equally dangerous. There had to be another way.

Frowning, he slowed his horse, turned him around and went back to the Goliad and Kansas intersection. He rode south to the jail.

He dismounted painfully and carried inside the three guns he had collected. He came back out, locked the door and stood still a moment, frowning and trying to decide what he should do.

The whole town knew how direct and undevious he was. Robineau, Sully, Moss and whoever else was waiting in the Gold Coin for him would expect him to come charging in the front door.

They knew his lightning speed with his gun and his deadly accuracy. Unwilling to trade even one of their lives for his, they'd have it arranged so they could blast him without risk to themselves the instant he burst through the door.

Well, he wouldn't play their game. He'd have to force them to come to him. The only trouble with that was that if Robineau failed to kill him himself, then he'd probably declare an open season on him and would offer a reward to whoever managed to bring him down.

All but three of Robineau's men still had guns. Furthermore, in a town like Cottonwood, guns were always available to anyone who wanted them badly enough.

So he'd have to move fast. Before the number of men who were dedicated to killing him grew any more.

CHAPTER 20

Morgan Gaunt stood there in the darkness in front of the jail for a long time, frowning, trying to work out some strategy that would succeed. He was betting now that all those who wanted to kill him were together in the Gold Coin Saloon. Quite possibly Kurt Vossler was also with them now.

He couldn't go in the front. That would be suicide. And it wouldn't work much better to go in the back. He could wait, of course, doing nothing, and hope they came out after him. But that course was fraught with risk. He wouldn't know where they were. All they'd have to do would be to wait until he appeared and then shoot him down.

Suddenly the worried expression on his face relaxed. There was a way. A way he thought would work.

251

He unlocked the jail and went in. He did not light the lamp. He took a double-barreled, sawed-off shotgun from the gun-rack and, with cartridges from his desk, loaded it. The cartridges were loaded with double-O buckshot. He stuck a handful of them into his pants pocket.

Carrying the gun, he went out into the darkness again and mounted his big chestnut, thinking with considerable regret that he might be sacrificing the animal, of which he was very fond, to save his own life. But there was no help for it.

In almost total darkness, he cut through the vacant lot beside the jail, in case they had a lookout watching for him, and rode up the alley behind it and the Pink Lady on the corner. When he reached Goliad, he could see the lighted, dirty windows of the Gold Coin and through them, the crowd inside.

He stopped, concealed beside the sagging, high board fence behind the Pink Lady. He watched the Gold Coin for almost five minutes. Nobody came or left. Further-more, little noise poured from the open door, not the usual yells of pure exuber-ance, not the tinkling sounds of a piano, not the shrill voices of women. They were waiting for him, all right.

He suddenly touched his heels to his horse's sides. The animal started across the street diagonally, straight toward the Gold Coin.

In Gaunt, every muscle, every nerve was tense. His leg ached ferociously from the strain he put on it, bracing it as he did against the stirrup. He kept the horse at a walk halfway across the street, his eyes alternately searching the shadows on both sides of the building and studying his horse's head and ears. He saw nothing and neither, apparently, did his horse. They were all inside, then. They had to be.

Straight for the door he rode, and when he reached the boardwalk, forced the horse up on it, heading straight for the swinging doors. The instant his horse's forefeet came down on the boardwalk with their distinctive sound, he whacked the horse across the rump with the barrel of the shotgun, at the same time leaving the saddle with a single smooth motion that put him on the boardwalk just in time to prevent his slamming against the side of the door.

The horse, lunging because of the surprising and unexpected whack on the rump, could not stop short of the door and went on into the saloon. Gaunt didn't wait to see what would happen then. He was already on his way around to the rear of the building, limping noticeably but now, in the excitement and tension of the moment, completely unaware of the pain.

Inside the saloon, a shotgun roared, its deep-throated sound echoed by several sharper pistol reports. Gaunt heard his horse's shrill nicker of terror. He heard the thunder of the horse's hoofs against the saloon floor and then he heard the shattering of glass as the horse leaped through one of the big front windows of the saloon. He heard the diminishing sounds of hoofs as the horse galloped down the street in the direction of either the stable or the jail.

Now he would see if his plan paid off. He figured that they'd expect him to be waiting in front of the saloon for them to come out.

If his calculations were right, not one of his intended assassins would go out the front of the saloon. They'd come charging out the back hoping to circle the building and cut him down from the shadows on each side.

He reached the corner of the building and rounded it at a run, revolver still in its holster, shotgun held in both his hands. He tripped on a pile of tin cans and went down with a crash that, he thought, could probably be heard for half a block. The shotgun, held in front of him, dug its muzzle into the ground.

Cursing soundlessly, Gaunt fought to his hands and knees. He supposed the shotgun was useless now. And so, probably, was his plan—unless, by some miraculous chance, the men inside had been making so much noise themselves they hadn't heard the crash he'd made falling over the pile of rusted cans.

As he froze there, listening, everything was silent except for the sound of booted feet on the floor inside the saloon. Gaunt stuck a finger into one bore of the shotgun and then the other one. His finger encountered some loose dirt adhering to the inside walls of the gunbarrel, but no solid plug of earth. He could use the gun, then, without blowing himself up.

The back door of the Gold Coin burst open and a man plunged out. Another came behind him and another still. Gaunt didn't dare wait for any more or these first three would be gone, hidden in the shadows. He roared, "Hold it! Don't take another step!"

A fourth and fifth man burst from the door before the first three could obey his command. Gaunt fired one barrel of the shotgun over their heads and three of the five men stopped. Two kept running and disappeared.

In the small amount of light streaming from the back door, Gaunt had recognized those two. Robineau and Moss. Sully had been the fifth man out. The remaining two looked like cowboys, but they both had guns.

All three men now whirled toward the sound of Gaunt's voice, their guns leveled, the hammers back. Gaunt roared, "Don't!" but he was too late. One of the cowboy's guns fired, the bullet taking out a chunk of board less than three inches from Gaunt's ear, a chunk that tore into his cheek and brought an instant rush of blood.

As always when he was hit, Gaunt's conscious mind ceased functioning. His reflexes took over without direction from his brain. The shotgun leveled and the second barrel roared. Buckshot rattled against the back wall of the Gold Coin Saloon.

One of the cowboys bent and grabbed his thigh, uttering a high cry of surprise and pain. The second doubled, clutching his belly. Sully, the last of the three, caught the bulk of the charge and fell without a sound.

No more men would be coming out the rear door now, Gaunt thought. But there were two, unhurt and deadly, probably less than fifty feet away from him. He broke the shotgun, the smell of powder smoke acrid in his nostrils, ejected the two spent cartridges and shoved two fresh ones in. He ran back to the front corner of the saloon, the shotgun ready in front of him.

Now he could go in, he thought. Robineau and Moss wouldn't do anything until they'd had time to figure out what had happened and what was likely to happen next. The biggest danger he faced inside the saloon would be from Kurt Vossler. The cowboys would most likely meekly surrender their guns, having seen what happened to the pair who had tried to bring the marshal down.

Without a moment's hesitation, Gaunt burst through the swinging door, a corner of his eye noticing the missing window on his left side as he did.

The place was a shambles. His horse, terrified at finding himself inside the noisy saloon, had knocked over half the tables and chairs in the place before he leaped through the big front window. Kurt Vossler was behind the bar, a shotgun lying on it, pointed toward the door.

Gaunt knew that shotgun would cut him in two if he didn't fire first. He leaped to one side, nearly falling because his wounded leg threatened to give way beneath him. The hammers of the shotgun were back.

No time to sweep the saloon with his glance for others who might have guns in their hands. He fired, and Vossler fired almost simultaneously.

Gaunt, his leg finally refusing to support him, fell just as he fired. Vossler's shotgun charge ripped the air over his head, taking out the window on the other side of the door from the one his horse had taken out earlier. Two of Vossler's buckshot, at the outer edge of the pattern, tore into the muscles of Gaunt's shoulder and stayed.

Flat on the floor, rolling, he saw Vossler driven back by the charge of his own gun. Vossler disappeared and Gaunt knew that he was already dead, having taken the full charge of buckshot in the face and chest.

There was broken glass all around him and every time he put a hand down it cut his palm. But he forced himself backward enough to feel the wall beneath the broken window at his back. He swept the shotgun around until it covered the surprised and frightened crowd. He roared angrily, "Anybody that has a gun, shed it. Now!"

In front there was a cowboy with a gun in his hand. There were a couple more with holstered guns at their sides. The three looked into the two gaping bores of the ten gauge and suddenly decided they had enough of their trail boss's fight. The man with the gun in his hand lowered the hammer and tossed it on the floor between him and Gaunt. The other two unbuckled their belts and tossed them after it.

Without lowering the hammer, and using the shotgun as a cane, Gaunt forced himself to his feet. The two pellets in his shoulder burned like fire, but there was little blood from the closely spaced wounds. He was mad now, hair-trigger mad, and the cowboys in the saloon saw his fury and watched him with eyes filled with fear. For all they knew he was still going to blast them with the shotgun at this close range.

He said angrily, "Every damn one of you stay right here! If I see one of you leave, I'll shoot to kill!"

He didn't wait for a reply. He picked

up the loose gun and the two holstered ones, turned and went outside, limping but scarcely aware of the pain. He was like a hunted, wounded and beleaguered animal, fighting desperately to survive.

Sully was dead. But there was still Robineau, who also had a shotgun, and Moss, armed with at least one gun and probably two. They were somewhere in the darkness. They might be hunting him separately or they might have joined forces.

More furious than he had ever been before in his life, he tramped along Goliad to Kansas Street and then south to the jail. He unlocked it, opened the door and threw the gun, belts and holsters inside. He locked the door again.

Turning, he saw the crowd that had gathered on the other side of Texas on Kansas Street. They were clustered on both sides, staring south toward the jail. They'd heard the revolver shots and the deep, booming shotgun blasts. He wished they weren't there because of the chance one of them might be hit by a stray bullet, but there was nothing he could do about them now. He had all he could do, keeping himself alive.

He paused for a moment in front of the

locked door of the jail. His plan for smoking them out of the Gold Coin Saloon had worked, but he had no other plan. How do you fight two men hidden by darkness just waiting for you to show yourself?

He supposed both Maggie Conover and Rose were in the crowd staring toward the jail, and he didn't want either of them to see him shot down.

Besides, he was the marshal. He was the law in Cottonwood. Come hell or high water, he wasn't going to skulk in alleys and vacant lots playing Robineau's and Moss's game.

With his mind made up, he turned and walked toward the stable. He went up the inclined ramp from the street, took down the lantern that hung just inside the door, struck a match and lighted it.

His chestnut was standing, trembling, in his stall. Gaunt walked back and led the animal out. Then, carefully, he went over the horse looking for wounds.

There were several glass cuts, all superficial, on the horse's chest. There was the previous wound on his rump. There was a shotgun pellet lodged in his neck, a lump beneath the skin and showing blue, but not serious unless it was pressing on a nerve.

Carefully he examined every square inch of the horse's body. He found no other wounds. The horse was all right. Only scared. Only stung, and skittish from his scare.

Talking soothingly to the horse, he put a boot into the stirrup and swung astride. Damn them, he thought, if they were going to kill him tonight, as least he was going down like a man. He rode down the ramp into the street.

The crowd still stood silently on both walks up on the other side of Texas Street. The pianos in the saloons were still. The shrill voices of the saloon girls and prostitutes were also still. There were no shouts. It was as if the town of Cottonwood was dead, or sound asleep.

Moss would shoot from ambush without warning, Gaunt thought. But Robineau, with his strange sense of pride that allowed him to use a shotgun to compensate for his crippled arm, would not be able to fire without first warning his victim that he intended to.

For a moment Gaunt sat his horse in the middle of Kansas Street, stroking the horse's neck and speaking soothingly to him. He knew the horse was so frightened and nervous that he might bolt at the slightest sound. That might be an advantage and it might not.

He touched the horse with his heels and moved on up the center of the street, starting his late-night rounds even though it was not yet late enough. The only way to smoke them out was to present himself as a target. A show of unconcern on his part could only make them more nervous than they already were.

He crossed Goliad and rode until he reached the Red Dog Saloon. Nobody seemed to be drinking inside of it. All were clustered at the windows and door, looking out.

A man came running down the street, and intercepted him just short of the Texas Street intersection. He yelled breathlessly, "You damn fool, are you trying to make it easier for him?" It was Lester Ives.

Gaunt said, "It's all right, Mr. Ives."

"What do you mean, it's all right? You're deliberately making a target of yourself!"

"Maybe. But how is it going to look if they make the law in Cottonwood run up and down back alleys like a rat?"

Ives made a disgusted exclamation.

Gaunt went on up Kansas Street, followed by Ives, and when he reached the crowd he said, "Get off the street, folks. There may be gunfire and one of you could be hit."

They began reluctantly to disperse. Gaunt rode on up the street. Rose was standing in the doorway of the Alamo, watching him, and she raised a hand. There was no sign of Maggie at her restaurant and the place was dark, but he had the feeling she was there, watching him, probably weeping and still trying to sort out in her own mind what she ought to do.

He reached Main and went on north, through the residential district of the town. He reached Hooker's hayfields, turned east and then rode south along the pitch-black, brushy bed of the creek.

He climbed out at the south end of town and entered the alleyway that separated the cattle pens. He was halfway when suddenly, directly ahead and in a pen on his right, a fire suddenly bloomed in a loose pile of hay.

It grew swiftly and in less than two seconds illuminated the whole area. So this was to be the place, Gaunt thought.

So rapidly did his mind work that he had

no consciousness of trying to figure this thing out. The gist of it was that one of them, probably Moss, had lighted the fire. Both Moss and Robineau were counting on him to whirl his horse and retreat. Or to leave his horse and try to find cover in one of the nearby pens.

If he retreated, he would be silhouetted against the fire as he came in range of Robineau's scattergun. If he went ahead, Moss could cut him down as he passed through the fire's light. If he dismounted and tried to hide, then both of them would hurry to the spot where he'd left his horse and hunt him down.

It looked like a damned good plan. And it might have worked except for the extreme nervousness of Gaunt's chestnut horse. As the fire grew, the horse suddenly and unexpectedly began to buck.

Gaunt could have ridden it out, despite his wounded leg. Instead, he chose to let the horse throw him and lit in the deep, dry manure beside one of the heavy cattle-pen fences. The shotgun roared, triggered by a surprised and already nervous Robineau, and Gaunt immediately fired at the muzzle flash.

Most of the shot rattled against the pen,

but one or two brought a grunt from Robineau. Hastily, Gaunt broke the shotgun, shoved in two fresh shells and instantly fired one barrel and then the second, at the same spot. There was one more shot from Robineau, his second barrel, but it was fired at the sky and Gaunt knew he'd gotten a solid hit.

He reloaded the shotgun, got to his feet, and ran as swiftly he could with his wounded leg, straight toward the fire in the pile of hay. A revolver shot flared across the alleyway, and that was all Gaunt needed. He stopped so quickly he nearly fell, set himself, and fired both shotgun barrels at his hidden ambusher.

Only after he had, did he become aware of a burning sensation along his ribs. And of the warm rush of blood.

He was hit again. But he could see Moss sprawled out on the ground. He opened the gate, went into the pen, and knelt at Moss's side. The man was dead.

Gaunt went back out into the alleyway and walked to where Robineau was. Robineau's chest was a mass of blood.

Gaunt heard the fire engine bell. He started toward his horse, now almost to the depot. Before he could reach the animal, the fire engine, drawn by a team of blacks, came rattling down Kansas Street headed toward the fire in the pens. Men in fire hats clung on behind and a gang of other men came running a couple of hundred yards behind.

Gaunt reached his horse and mounted him. He headed uptown. At the Alamo, Rose stepped out into the street and barred his way. "You get down and come in here. I'll send for the doctor. Let him come to you this time."

There was something authoritative in her voice, but it had a pleading quality as well. Gaunt got off his horse. He was suddenly very tired, and it didn't seem as if there were many places that didn't hurt.

He tied his horse. Rose took his arm and helped him inside. He climbed the stairs with her.

Inside her room, she insisted that he lie down, dirty clothes and all, on her bed. She sat beside him and looked into his face.

Gaunt said, "It will be all right now. For the rest of the year."

Her eyes were large, very serious and questioning. He said, "I'm going to break it off with Maggie."

"Why?"

"I'd like to marry you. If you'll have me."

Tears came like a flood into her eyes. She put her face down against his chest and wept until she heard the doctor coming up the stairs. She raised her head then and in response to his questioning glance, nodded her head vigorously.

He thought that it didn't really matter what he did. If he had Rose, he'd be happy doing anything. He felt guilty about Maggie briefly, and then even that went away.

The publishers hope that this Large Print Book has brought you pleasurable reading. Each title is designed to make the text as easy to see as possible. G. K. Hall Large Print Books are available from your library and your local bookstore. Or you can receive information on upcoming and current Large Print Books by mail and order directly from the publisher. Just send your name and address to:

G. K. Hall & Co.
70 Lincoln Street
Boston, Mass. 02111

A note on the text
Large print edition designed by
Lyda Kuth.
Composed in 18 pt English Times
on a CompuWriter II
by Adhanet Elias.